"Hey, don't cry. It's going to be all right."

Daniel Riverton put his arms underneath her. She could smell the crisp, clean scent of him, and feel the banded muscle of his arms as he slid them beneath her.

For a moment, Trixie had to shut her eyes against a wave of dizziness. When she opened them, she expected she would have a more realistic perspective of her rescuer.

Instead, her first impression deepened. Now she could see him fully, and he really was the most mouthwatering man she had ever seen.

She knew he really was incredibly, heart-stoppingly handsome. Add to that her every sense tingling with that blissful awareness of life's glories that a close brush with catastrophe could bring? Daniel Riverton was irresistible.

"Please stop crying. I've got you."

Dear Reader,

I have now lived away from Calgary much longer than I ever lived there. But I was born and raised there, my sisters live there, and I will always consider it my hometown. Calgary is famous for the Stampede and never far from its Western roots. The last time I used the airport in Calgary, a flight was boarding at a different gate. The airline attendant came on the public address system, and said, "We're in Calgary, so no one is getting on that plane until I hear a big yahoo." I kind of smiled to myself, and thought, *That will never happen.*

The "yahoo" was deafening. People who *weren't* getting on that flight shouted it out, Calgary's signature greeting, an enthusiastic affirmation of all that city is: vibrant, young, energetic and fun.

Shortly after I finished writing this book, Calgary and the surrounding areas, particularly High River, suffered the most shattering floods in the history of Alberta. It was heartbreaking to see the damage and devastation. And then inspiring to watch people find their true spirit, rise to the challenge, help one another, become better instead of bitter. The Calgary Stampede went on, two weeks after the flood, with the motto Come Hell or High Water. My hat is off to the everyday heroes of my hometown!

If you live in Calgary, or just love it there, come visit me on Facebook and we'll swap stories.

Until then, I hope you enjoy meeting Daniel and Trixie, and the two incorrigible (but adorable) Aussie twins, Molly and Pauline.

Yahoo!

Cara

Rescued by the Millionaire

Cara Colter

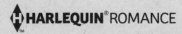
HARLEQUIN® ROMANCE

ISBN-13: 978-0-373-74277-6

RESCUED BY THE MILLIONAIRE

First North American Publication 2014

Copyright © 2014 by Cara Colter

Printed in U.S.A.

Cara Colter lives in British Columbia with her partner, Rob, and eleven horses. She has three grown children and a grandson. She is a recent recipient of an *RT Book Reviews* Career Achievement Award in the Love and Laughter category.

Also by Cara Colter

SNOWFLAKES AND SILVER LININGS*
HOW TO MELT A FROZEN HEART
SECOND CHANCE WITH THE REBEL**
SNOWED IN AT THE RANCH
BATTLE FOR THE SOLDIER'S HEART
THE COP, THE PUPPY AND ME
TO DANCE WITH A PRINCE
RESCUED BY HIS CHRISTMAS ANGEL
WINNING A GROOM IN 10 DATES
RESCUED IN A WEDDING DRESS

*The Gingerbread Girls
**Mothers in a Million

This and other titles by Cara Colter are available in ebook format at www.Harlequin.com.

To my friend Debbie Kepke, who put the "try" in triathlon.
Thanks for allowing me to be part of the journey.

CHAPTER ONE

THE PITTER-PATTER of little feet.

Daniel Riverton lay on the sofa contemplating that saying with utter dislike. It seemed to him he had always heard that expression spoken with affection, usually by his mother who seemed to hold out the hope, despite all the evidence to the contrary—and her considerable contribution to his cynicism about romance—that he was going to provide her with grandchildren someday.

His mother. Twenty-two text messages today. Who on earth had taught her to text, anyway?

Urgent. Please call. Are you avoiding me?

At least the pitter-patter of little feet was providing something of a distraction from *that*. But obviously that expression would never be used with affection by anyone who had tried living below apartment 602 Harrington Place for the past four days.

Obviously that expression would never be used, period, by anyone being subjected to the actual pitter-patter of little feet. At three in the morning, when the owners of said little feet should be in bed, fast asleep.

As far as Daniel could tell, the owners of said little feet had woken up at about the same time he was getting home from a long, productive and wonderfully challenging day of avoiding his mother's phone calls and looking after business at his company, River's Edge Enterprises. Today, he had put in fourteen hours, had a light dinner with friends and come home just wanting the most simple of pleasures: a good night's sleep.

At two in the morning he had moved from his bedroom after it had become evident the little monsters from upstairs were jumping on a bed located somewhere directly above his head.

But the pitter-patter of little feet had followed him. For the past hour they had been running in a frantic, tight circle right above his new location on the sofa. The light fixture above him—*Swarovski,* apparently—was trembling and shuddering ominously.

The condominium manager, Mrs. Bulittle, had been unsympathetic about his complaints.

"Yes, Mr. Riverton, it *is* an adult only building, but people *are* allowed to have children visit."

This said as if he, Daniel, the victim of the pitter-pattering, was the nuisance, as if he had said children shouldn't be allowed in the world, not asked for the right to quiet enjoyment in his own premises, heavy emphasis on the quiet.

Temporary premises, thank goodness. The Harrington was an older building, surrounded with lilacs, rather than the more modern aesthetic for landscaping. Still, it had a sought-after southwest Calgary location right on the edge of lower Mount Royal.

The circa 1970 apartments had been converted to condos. Despite Kevin's extravagant upgrades to this unit, it was more than evident no one had given soundproofing a thought back in the good old days.

Was it even possible to soundproof against such an onslaught?

While he was feeling annoyed with expressions, Daniel decided to add "never look a gift horse in the mouth" to his list. Three in the morning was a great time to compile lists of trivial sayings *and* to look gift horses in the mouth.

It had seemed serendipitous when his best friend Kevin Wilson, owner of 502, had been going overseas on a photography assignment for three months at the very same time Daniel's own premises—a very upscale loft conversion that was completely soundproof—was undergoing a major renovation.

At the very same time he was going into hiding from his mother.

He owned the building. His loft apartment was right above his business, and he was the only person who lived in the building, a fact he would be a great deal more grateful for when he returned to it.

He'd been talked into the renovation when he'd been seeing an interior designer, Angelica. He'd already known they weren't going anywhere as a couple, and so had she. They both had extraordinarily demanding professional lives—the pitter-patter of little feet not even a blip on either of their radars—but he had liked the bachelor chic of her design, a design notably lacking a Swarovski crystal chandelier.

The renovation had now outlasted the relationship by several weeks. The breakup had been amiable, as were most of his breakups.

When he had complained to the manager about the noise in 602 for the third time, Mrs. Bulittle had sniffed and said, "It's not as if Mr. Wilson hasn't had a noisy party or two."

Daniel was pretty sure he'd heard the slightest touch of smugness in her voice, which was possible since Mrs. Bulittle lived directly below 502, in 402.

She had no doubt suffered a night or two of lost sleep herself, since Daniel could vouch for the noisiness of several parties he had attended in this very apartment.

Ah, he and Kevin had enviable lives. Successful thirtysomethings, unattached, and pretty much devoted to keeping it that way, much to the chagrin of both their mothers!

Daniel, where are you staying during the reno of your loft? I can't reach you. Is this any way to treat your mother?

Mom, I'm fine. Just busy.

He followed that with a couple of heart symbols. He liked texting! You could have the pretext of intimacy while being totally disengaged. To assuage the slight guilt he was feeling for avoiding her, he sent her flowers, thanking his lucky stars that her marriage to Pierre had landed her in Montreal and she loved it there and still lived there. If she was local and lacking his current address? She would be camped out in his office!

* * *

Kevin was an internationally known photographer, Daniel the head of River's Edge. His company was a software engineering firm that had developed some of the best technologies used in the Alberta oil fields.

In recent years, Daniel had applied his considerable ambition and business acumen to real estate, and investing in young companies that he thought had potential. So he was *not* accustomed to being brushed off by a building manager, who had told him, with a certain mean satisfaction, "I'll give you the tenant's name and phone number. You talk to her."

The *her* in question was Patricia Marsh. When Daniel called, he had to shout to make himself heard over the caterwauling in the background. She'd sounded harried, exhausted and she had been totally apologetic. Her nieces were visiting. They were from Australia, the difference in times meant they were having trouble settling into a normal routine.

She had promised changes, and Patricia Marsh had possessed one of those lovely, husky voices that might have inspired belief in one less jaded than himself. He had ended the call on a curt note—probably more because of being harassed by his mother than anything to do with Patricia Marsh—but oh, well.

None of the promised changes had materialized, so he was less and less sorry for the curt note.

It was day four   make that night four—in the combat zone. There was sudden silence above his head, but instead of enjoying it, Daniel noted that his headache felt permanent, and his shoulders were bunched up with tension.

So, the visiting children were having a little break right now. He wished he could appreciate the silence, and he tried to. He closed his eyes, willed himself back to sleep.

He was closing the Bentley deal tomorrow. Months of groundwork were coming to fruition. He needed to be razor-sharp and ready. He needed his sleep. But instead of sleeping, he contemplated the silence with deep suspicion, like a soldier waiting for the firing to start again.

Five minutes. Then ten. Then fifteen. At half an hour of blissful silence, he took a deep breath, and allowed himself to be lulled into a sense of security. The knot in his forehead relaxed ever so slightly and he felt his shoulders unwind.

Tomorrow, he'd go get a hotel for the duration of the children's visit. He'd been to that nice boutique hotel across from the Bow River at the invitation of a visiting female executive a few years back. They had luxurious, quiet suites. He remembered there were great jogging paths at Prince's Island. He could run in the morning before he went to the office—

His eyes closed. Ahhh. Bliss.

Trixie Marsh's eyes fluttered open, and for a moment she just felt the utter contentment of having rested. But the moment was fleeting.

It was very dark in her apartment. Was she sitting up? She felt deeply disoriented.

The twins! She had not rested properly since the arrival of her four-year-old nieces.

Even as she'd worried about her own twin sister Abby's seemingly impulsive plan to drop off her children, she had been thrilled to have time with Molly and Pauline. She had envisioned finger painting and building with Play-Doh, romps in the park and bedtime stories. Trixie had envisioned time with the twins as a glimpse at the life she always wanted for herself.

And really she should have known better! The life she had always wanted for herself was really the life she had always had growing up: surrounded by family and laughter, a sense of safety and belonging.

Always had, until her parents had been killed in a car accident the year she had graduated from high school. Since then, it seemed the more she chased after what had once been, the more it eluded her like a ghostly vision, growing dimmer with each passing day of her life.

As it turned out, her nieces preferred their finger painting on the walls. And on each other's faces. And on the cat. They liked eating Play-Doh and they *loved* that this unusual dietary choice made for very colorful poop.

They didn't listen to Trixie *ever*, they were up all night and the man in the apartment below her—it couldn't be *that* Daniel Riverton, could it?—was complaining. In a voice so sexy it made Trixie's heart hurt!

"Enough," she snapped at herself, out loud. It occurred to her it *was* night and her apartment was eerily silent.

Plus *enough* did not come out *enough*. It came out a garbled *eblubluk*. There was something in her mouth. It felt almost as if her cat, Freddy, a long-haired Persian, was nestled close to her face. She went to brush him away.

And that's when Trixie realized she was trapped. Her arms wouldn't move. And neither would her legs.

Suddenly, panic rising, it came back to her.

"Auntie," Molly said, blinking her huge brown eyes at her, "this is our favorite game. Our mommy lets us play it. You sit in the chair, and Pauline and I go around and around you with the roll of toilet tissue."

It had seemed harmless enough. And quiet, too. What she had not been counting on was the almost hypnotic effect of her nieces moving silently around and around her, pink tongues caught between little teeth in concentration.

What she hadn't realized was the depths of her own exhaustion, and how relieved she was that they were being quiet.

What she hadn't realized was that enough of that tissue could bind like steel. It wasn't just tissue. She could taste the fluff of quilting batting in her mouth.

Frantically, Trixie pulled at her limbs. She was stuck fast to the chair.

Endless scenarios began to run through her head. None of them had a happy ending. She was going to die. She just knew it. Her whole life was flashing before her eyes: she and Abby growing up in their matching clothes, unwrapping gifts at the Christmas tree, baking cookies with their mother, at the cottage…and then the knock on the door.

So sorry, an accident.

And Abby marrying and moving to Australia.

And Trixie being so alone.

And so when Miles, her one and only boyfriend, had said, *Move in with me, I'll look after you,* there had been no choice involved, really.

And when he left, he hadn't given her a choice, either.

For a moment, she pictured him bursting through the door, rescuing her, admitting the error of his ways, giving her back her dreams.

Trixie blinked hard. That's how she had gone through her whole life. Acting like someone else was in charge of her dreams. Acting as though she had no choice.

Now was she going to die the same way? As if she was powerless? As if she had no choice. No! She was going to fight and fight hard.

It wasn't just about her. Her nieces were in peril, too. They could all perish here if Trixie didn't act and act quickly.

She began to rock the chair.

Bang.

It sounded like an explosion, not a subdued pop, more like a mortar round had gone off right in Daniel's trench. Whatever had hit the floor above his head had hit it so loudly the crystals in the chandelier clanged against each other dangerously. Daniel jumped up off the sofa, his heart beating fast.

IIe waited for the sound of running feet to start again.

Nothing.

The hair on the back of his neck rose. And he knew, to the pit of his stomach, something was wrong upstairs, in the apartment above him.

He paused only at his own door to shove shoes on his bare feet and then Daniel raced out of his apartment, down the hallway and up the steps.

Outside 602, he asked himself what he was doing. If he was so sure something was wrong, why not call 911?

And say what? I was busy composing a list of inane sayings and then, guess what? *I heard a bump in the night!*

He stood outside the door for a moment, listening. He found the silence eerie, and the hair on the back of his neck would not sit down. He knocked on the door. There it was—the pitter-patter of running little feet. But nothing else. No other sounds, including the one he was listening for, the husky, lovely notes of an adult voice, someone in charge.

He knocked again, louder, more insistent.

After a long pause, and more of the pitter-patter, the door handle squeaked. The door slid open two inches, catching on the chain lock.

Nobody appeared to be there.

And then he looked down.

Two identical solemn faces, smeared with tears and what appeared to be red berry juice, were pressed against the crack in the doorway, and the tiny girls regarded him warily.

"Is your, uh, mommy here?"

"Mama goned."

The Australian accent was noticeable. It looked like they were going to close the door.

"Aunt!" he remembered. "Is your aunt Patricia here?"

"Auntie's name Trixie."

He was starting to feel exasperated, but a sound from in the apartment, muted, but very much like a whimper, made the hair on the back of his neck stand up higher.

"Get your aunt for me," he said, trying for a note of both sternness, to instill obedience, and friendliness to try and overcome whatever they had heard about the danger of strangers.

Two sets of identical liquid dark eyes exchanged a look.

"She's dead," one offered.

"Unlock the door. Right now." He fumbled for his cell phone, always in his shirt pocket, and realized he wasn't even in a shirt. He was standing in the hallway in a pair of plaid pajama bottoms, and his best shoes and nothing else.

Not exactly the person children would or should unlock the door for.

"Please?" He tried for a sweet note. It came as unnaturally to him as if he was speaking through the sickening fluff of candy floss. He tried to smile in a friendly fashion.

The children were fooled—it made him uncomfortably aware of how totally vulnerable children were—and one of them ventured a tiny smile in return while the other stood on tiptoes and tried to reach the chain that barred the door.

"Can't reach." And that was that. The little minx looked as if, now that she had made somewhat of an effort, she was going to shut the door.

"Get out of the way," he ordered. "Stand way back from the door."

The pitter-patter of running feet told him he had, somewhat surprisingly, been obeyed. Either that, or they had totally lost interest in him and run off to play. He threw his shoulder into the door, and the flimsy chain snapped with barely a protest, and the door crashed open and hit the coat closet door behind it with an explosive bang. Daniel was propelled into the darkness of the apartment.

A huge cat, long haired and gray, shot out of the closet, yowling with indignation. White fluff, an inch deep on the floors, floated in the air behind the cat as it skittered around a corner and disappeared into one of the bedrooms.

Daniel could only hope one of the neighbors

had heard the ruckus and would have the good sense to call for help.

"Patricia?" he called. "Patricia Marsh? It's Daniel Riverton, your neighbor from downstairs."

He heard that little whimper again. The layout of the apartment was identical to Kevin's, so he got his bearings, moved swiftly past the kitchen and down the short hallway. He burst into the living room. His every step seemed to stir clouds of *something* off the floor.

The children, obviously identical twins, sat in complete darkness on a brightly patterned sofa by the window, peering at something they held between them.

"Don't be frightened," he said. One of them glanced up at him with a look that appeared defiant, not the least frightened.

He wasn't sure about kids' ages, since children were the segment of the population that, thankfully, he had the least to do with. He thought maybe these little girls were four or five.

They were dressed in identical white nighties, but that was where any perception of innocence ended. Their hair was black, wildly curly, long and tangled. They looked like children who had been raised by wolves.

As if to underscore that perception, one lifted up her bright red hand, berry-stained like her face, and licked it.

"Where's your aunt?"

Despite the fact the layout of the apartment was identical to Kevin's, Daniel found himself feeling disoriented by the mess. It seemed as if it had snowed inside. That white fluff was everywhere. It covered the floor, and floated in little clumps. A closer glance showed him dozens of envelopes were scattered, like so much debris, among the disarray.

Just off the living room, in the dining room alcove, in the middle of that sea of mail and white fluff, was an overturned dining chair.

With a mummy attached to it. Again, the scene was so surreal, he felt disoriented, his mind grappling with what was going on.

Then mummy whimpered.

Daniel raced over and dropped to his knees. All that was visible through one tiny slat in layers and layers of white—toilet tissue?—were the most incredible eyes he had ever seen, as midnight blue as the heart of a pansy, fringed with dark lashes that had teardrops that sparkled like diamonds clinging to them.

He said a word out loud that he was pretty

sure you weren't supposed to say in front of children.

Even ones who looked like little ruffians straight off the set of *Oliver Twist*.

CHAPTER TWO

Trixie Marsh saw his shoes first. They were, without a doubt, the most beautiful sight she had ever seen. And it wasn't just because the shoes were Berluti either.

And Trixie knew shoes. She had knelt in front of thousands and thousands of pairs of very good quality men's shoes, patiently pinning the hemlines of trousers, handmade by her former employer, Bernard Brothers—Miles's family's business—one of the most sought after makers of custom men's clothing in Calgary.

Daniel Riverton—she would have known it was him, because of the shoes, even if he hadn't announced himself at the door—crouched down beside her.

This was a first! Reality better than a dream! Because she had dreamed of being rescued by Miles, and really there was no comparison. None at all.

Miles, was, well, ordinary. Daniel Riverton, was, well, not ordinary.

His eyes intensified her feeling that she was experiencing beauty as she never had before. They were a color deeper than sapphire, the astounding blue of deep, deep ocean water.

But it was the fact they were tinged with concern, and a certain take-charge expression, that made her gasp—muffled as it was by the bindings over her mouth—with heartfelt wonder. Just as she had been contemplating death, the knock had come on the door. It was like a fairy tale: a knight rescuing a maiden from an ignoble fate.

"Hey, don't cry. It's going to be all right."

Again, her feeling of being in an altered state, where everything glowed from within, intensified. His voice was astounding, deep and sexy and a little rough around the edges. And it wasn't because she knew it belonged to one of the most up and coming businessmen in Canada, either!

It was because she had spent the past half hour contemplating all the dreadful possibilities that could result from the pickle she had found herself in.

It was only because he was her rescuer, her knight, her prince, that her every sense was on high alert, that she found his voice so unbelievably sensuous. Wasn't it?

As she lay there, helpless to do anything but try to blink back tears, wrapped head to toe in tissue and gauze that held her fast to her overturned chair, Daniel Riverton put his arms underneath her. She could smell the crisp, clean scent of him, and even through the thick layers of tissue, she could feel the banded muscle of his arms as he slid them beneath her. With easy strength he righted the chair.

For a moment, Trixie had to shut her eyes against a wave of dizziness. When she opened them, she expected she would have a more realistic perspective of her rescuer.

Instead, her first impression deepened. Now, she could see him fully, and he really was the most mouthwatering man she had ever seen.

She knew he really was incredibly, heartstoppingly handsome. Add to that her every sense tingling with that blissful awareness of life's glories that a close brush with catastrophe could bring? Daniel Riverton was irresistible.

"Please stop crying. I've got you."

Again, the words seemed to shine, to be illuminated, as beautiful as any she had ever heard.

I've got you.

It wasn't just that she had felt in way over her head since the arrival of her nieces. Even before that, she had been blindsided by Miles opting out of her dreams for the two of them.

She could still picture him frowning at her new bedroom curtains, soft white lace, saying *This just isn't what I want.*

What isn't to want? Trixie had cried. Begged as he packed his things, something grimly determined on his face, *They're only curtains.*

But it obviously had not been about the curtains.

So, Trixie was trying to adjust to single life, trying get her fledgling business off the ground, feeling like she was back to square one, as alone as she had been since her parents died.

But this time determined to see her independence as an asset.

"I've got you," Daniel said again, and the words were a shameful relief to someone who was determined to see independence as an asset!

His hand rested on her mummified shoulder, but even through all the layers and layers of padding, Trixie could feel something faintly electrical in his touch, something beyond strength and confidence.

She nodded, and willed the tears to quit spilling, but they wouldn't. She saw her nieces sitting on the sofa, and the tears spilled harder.

She had unwittingly put them in harm's way. Some aunt she was!

"You look like the tire man in that commercial," he said, attempting levity, probably because her tears were making him uncomfortable. When she had spoken to him on the phone he had sounded like a man who would be uncomfortable with tears—and she'd been close to crying then, too.

"You know the one?" he went on, in that deep, unconsciously seductive, comforting voice. "He's totally made of tires? Only his eyes look out?"

She sniffled and swallowed, so trapped she could not even wipe her own nose. It was that thought—her helplessness in the face of nasal dribbles, as much as his attempt at lightness—that made her choke back more tears.

"Or maybe the Bisquitboy." He was definitely trying to calm her, and his voice was intentionally without hard edges, soothing. "You know the one? He giggles when someone sticks a finger in his paunch?"

Of course she knew who the tire man was! And the pudgy little dough man. Trixie had always considered them both quite cute, but that was before she had been compared to them! But being seen as the tire man, or worse, the Doughboy, was humiliating on your first encounter with a devastatingly attractive man, even as his voice and presence strove to reassure.

Daniel Riverton was inspecting her carefully, trying to figure out where to start unraveling her.

One magazine had dubbed him Calgary's most eligible bachelor.

Not that she should care! The last thing Trixie was in the market for was a man in her life. She was barely finding her feet after the breakup—make that *dumping*, a little voice in her head insisted—with Miles.

Still, even if you weren't in the market, you'd have to be unconscious not to feel that little shiver of *something* in the presence of a man like Daniel Riverton, especially Daniel Riverton, in rescue mode, with no shirt on. Her eyes lingered on his bare chest.

Deep and smooth, golden, as if he had recently been somewhere warm.

The nearly naked Daniel Riverton decided on a starting point by her ear. He tried to rip through the layers of padded white.

"That's stronger than I would have believed," he muttered, and began to unwind the binding from around her head.

He was so close to her. She could see the amazing flawlessness of his skin. His scent—

clean, masculine, sensual—tickled at her nostrils despite the fact they were still covered in several layers of tissue.

"Get me a pair of scissors," he snapped at Molly and Pauline. His voice, to them, was brusque, but the quick efficiency with which he was unwrapping Trixie remained gentle.

"Not allowed—"

That would be Molly, always the leader of the shenanigans.

"Now you *are* allowed," he said sternly.

Molly wasn't about to let that go without challenging it. "Are you the boss over me?"

"You're damned right I am," he said. It was definitely the voice of a man who led a successful company and commanded dozens of employees, but Molly cocked her head at him, and narrowed her eyes.

But even a four-year-old could not miss the fact he was not a man to be messed with. She gave in with surprising ease. She slid off the sofa, followed by the ever faithful Pauline. Trixie heard them move a chair across the kitchen floor and start to dig in a drawer.

"So," he said, his voice once again even and threaded with just a hint of amusement, "The mystery begins to unravel. What color of hair is that?"

"Auburn," Trixie tried to say, hoping he had

unraveled enough layers from around her face
that he could hear her. It came out mumbo
jumbo.

He frowned in concentration. "What?"

She tried again.

"Aw bum? Oh! All brown? With those big
blue eyes, I expected you to be blonde. No, wait,
I can see your hair now. It's not all brown. It's
reddish, like whiskey aged in a sherry cask."

Whiskey aged in a sherry cask? Good grief!
This man knew his way around women. As if
she hadn't already guessed that!

He was talking slowly and continuously, as if
he could sense the panic in her was still close to
the surface, as if he had happened upon someone on the edge of a rooftop, and it was his
voice that could talk them away from the edge.

He had to ruin her relishing the whiskey-aged
description of her hair, by adding, "Your hair
probably doesn't usually stick out every which
way, like this. It looks like you stuck your finger in a socket. Ouch! It is shooting off static,
too."

Trixie had recently had her long hair cut to
a shorter length, mistakenly thinking that it
would take less work. Instead, if it wasn't tack-
led with a straight iron her hair looked very
much like a gone-to-seed dandelion, waiting
for someone to blow.

Now, her hair crackled under his touch as he unwound the tissue and batting from it.

"Electricity between us," he said in that same mild, get-away-from-the-ledge tone of voice. Again, the light, teasing tone reminded her that he knew his way around women. So did the playful, faintly villainous wagging of the dark arrows of his brows.

But Trixie also knew he was one hundred per cent joking because there was no undoing a first impression. The tire man. The Doughboy. Someone whose hair looked as if they had stuck their finger in an electrical outlet.

"You have remarkably tiny ears," he continued his calm narration. "Pierced, but no earrings. I wonder what kind of earrings you would wear? I'm going to guess nothing too flashy. Small diamond studs, perhaps?"

More like cubic zirconia, but if he wanted to picture her in diamonds, she'd take it as a bit of a counterpoint to the finger-in-the-socket remark.

She knew he was keeping up the one-sided conversation for her benefit only, and it did have a calming effect on her.

"Peaches and cream complexion, nose like a little button, no make-up. But if you did wear it? I'd guess a light dusting."

Again, that sense that he knew way too much about women!

He had unwound enough of the tissue that he could stop unwinding and tear the remainder away from her face.

He regarded her with a surprised half smile tickling his lips. "And no bright red lipstick on those lips. They are quite luscious without it. In fact, I take it back. You look nothing like the tire man. Or the Doughboy." His eyes moved to her hair, and the half smile deepened to a full one. "The electrical socket we can do nothing about."

Her arms and hands pulled against the bindings. She was dying to pat her hair into place, but she was still bound fast. And aware, from the effort of trying to move, that something was wrong with her shoulder.

Still, she brushed that aside and gulped in a deep, appreciative breath of air. She wasn't sure if she should say thanks, but before she had decided, he dropped the chatter and was briskly all business.

"Are you hurt?"

"Mostly my pride." Her voice was a croak.

"Mostly?"

"My shoulder hurts," she confessed, clearing her throat. "But not as much as my pride. I feel horribly stupid. Horribly."

No, stupid did not cut it. She would have felt stupid if her neighbor, the lovely elderly Miss Twining had found her.

But to be found in this situation by Daniel Riverton?

While he was definitely the rescuer straight out of a dream, it was still absolutely mortifying. His picture had been gracing the cover of major business magazines for at least a year, including *Calgary Entrepreneur* which she subscribed to, and read avidly from cover to cover, since starting her own small business after being let go—*fired,* her mind supplied helpfully—from Bernard Brothers a year ago.

"What on earth happened in here?"

When he had introduced himself on the phone a few days ago, she had denied it could be *that* Daniel Riverton.

But, now with him standing in front of her, in the flesh—literally, she glanced greedily at his naked chest again—there was no denying it. And nothing—certainly not looking at his picture on the cover of a magazine, or listening to his admittedly quite sexy, if irritated, voice on the phone—could have prepared her for the man.

Maybe it was good she was tied to a chair. In her weakened state, four days with her nieces and now running on pure panic and adrenalin for the past hour—plus debilitating pain was shooting through her shoulder and arm—it was probably all that was preventing her from swooning.

Because he was literally in the flesh—his arms sleek and lightly muscled, his naked chest broad, and smooth, without a hair marring the silk of his skin, his pajama pants dipping very low on his hips, showing her that place where hard abs narrowed below his belly button, to an enticing *V* that made her mouth go dry.

No! she insisted on lying to herself, her mouth was already stuffed-with-cotton dry.

He had black hair, which looked impossibly well groomed even though he had obviously been in bed. And he had features so perfect it could have been the cover of *GQ* he had posed for rather than business magazines.

Or, with that perfect naked chest, one of those calendars that featured gorgeous men leaning on fire trucks or carrying saddles.

Trixie made herself look away from *that,* not that the perfect features of his face provided respite from the awareness of him that was thrumming through her veins.

Why did she feel faintly, ridiculously guilty that Miles had never made her feel this way? Miles had never rescued her from certain death, that was why!

Still, Miles with his pasty complexion and shock of thinning red hair, with his cute little tummy and pudgy limbs had been the antithesis of this man.

Daniel had high cheekbones, a perfectly shaped nose, a firm mouth saved from arrogance by the plumpness of his lower lip, a chin that was square and faintly dimpled.

His cheeks and chin were ever so faintly shadowed with dark whiskers, which added to, rather than detracted from, how gorgeous he was.

But it was his eyes that were absolutely mesmerizing. The magazine cover had not captured the true blue of them.

Trixie wondered, and hated herself for wondering, was this tingling awareness of Daniel the "something more" that Miles had left her in search of?

He began to unravel the rest of her binding, his way no-nonsense and firm. "There's got to be a dozen rolls of paper on you."

Trying to ignore the heated sensation being caused by his hands unraveling tissue from very personal places—that sizzling awareness of something more— Trixie tried to focus. He wanted to know what happened. Stick with the facts, ma'am!

"I was just so tired," she said. "They never

sleep. They're from Australia. I mean Molly and Pauline are in a completely different time zone, as I told you."

"And as I could not help but notice!" This said a touch grimly.

"It was your phone call that made me so anxious to not be noisy. I had just gone to sleep. They woke me up jumping on the bed. Then they wanted to eat. Then they wanted to play this game.

"They said their mother let thcm play it all the time. I was to sit in a chair, and they would wrap me in toilet tissue. I just didn't see the harm. I was desperate to keep them quiet."

For you.

Even though she hadn't said it out loud a sardonic smile touched the glorious curve of his mouth. "Ah, yes, the complaining neighbor."

"Not that I was blaming you," she said hastily.

"That's good."

"Though you were very intimidating on the phone." He was still very intimidating. So she tossed her head and added, like a woman not easily intimidated, "And a little rude."

"I get that way when I'm sleep deprived. So, if you could just continue with your little story."

Her little story? She was beginning to find her rescuer a bit aggravating. He was just one of those men. So supremely self-confident, so sure in his own skin, that it grated slightly. Daniel Riverton was a man who compared a woman's hair to whiskey, and guessed at her earrings, as a matter of course.

Still, she did, possibly, owe him her life, so an explanation was in order.

"So they were going around and around me, each of them with their own roll of tissue. They were concentrating very hard, and they were being very quiet, for once, and I was very grateful for that. But it was terribly hypnotic. I must have nodded off. I can't believe I did that! But I've been working all day, and up all night with them, since they arrived, and I just drifted off. And when I woke up, I was trapped. I couldn't believe how strong it was. You'd think you could just rip through tissue, but, as you can see they got into my quilting stuff, too—"

She was blathering and she noticed he was more focused on the task of releasing her than her "little story." She shut her mouth with a snap. The twins, finally, arrived with a pair of scissors and he made quick work of the rest of the bindings, seemingly not even noticing that she had stopped talking.

She watched the dark silkiness of his hair as he bent over her, cutting away the twins' handi-work. As she had suspected, it wasn't just tissue. He cut through quilting batting as well. Sometime after she'd gone to sleep, the twins had helped themselves to things from her workroom. She noticed an inch of white fluff floated above the floor of the entire living room and knew they had finally succeeded in getting into her bags of cotton stuffing.

Since they had arrived they had been begging her to play with the bags of *snow.*

And the envelopes—orders—that she had stacked so neatly on her desk, afraid to open them, were strewn from one end of the apartment to the other. She groaned, and he followed her gaze.

"You get a great deal of mail," he said. He stooped and picked up an envelope. "It's addressed to Cat in the Hat. What's that about? Your hair?"

"My hair?"

"Sorry." He grinned with apologetic charm. "It does kind of have that wet cat look about it. A wet cat pulled from a hat."

"I thought it looked like I put my finger in an electrical socket."

"I'm rethinking it," he said, regarding her so intently she could feel heat burning up her cheeks. "A wet cat who stuck its paw in a socket?"

"Oh! Is it that bad?"

"I'm just teasing you. Sorry."

She was being teased by *the* Daniel Riverton? Life certainly had some unexpected twists and turns in it. She contemplated this one. She contemplated that she seemed to like being teased.

Her relationship with Miles could not have been called playful. And she hadn't been aware, until this very moment, that that was a lack.

He brushed a hand over his eyes and apologized again. "You aren't the only one who is exhausted." He cast a look of unveiled annoyance at her nieces. "So why are you getting mail addressed to the Cat in the Hat?"

"It's a long story." For a delirious moment she pictured herself pouring it out to him. Who better to share it with? A successful businessman—

"Perhaps another time, then," he said with utter insincerity, reminding her of the arrogance right under the surface of all the charm…and teasing. "I think we've got you free, Miss Cat-in-the-Hat."

And that would be his cue to leave, and never glance back. Certainly, he would not want to hear about all her production woes with a company that would be so teeny next to his it would be like a mouse standing beside an elephant.

No, closer to a flea.

"You are surprisingly tiny under all that,"

he said, letting an enormous ball of tissue drop from his hands as he inspected her. "At least I think you are."

Despite the fact her freedom meant she would probably never see her neighbor again, Trixie was relieved beyond belief to be loose, and even more relieved that she had on a perfectly respectable, if somewhat bulky, housecoat that she had made herself.

The housecoat might have left her tininess in question, and made her want to call out her weight to him as further proof she was not in any way related to the Doughboy. But this situation could have been even more horrible if she hadn't had it on. What if she'd been sitting here in her pajamas, a pair of boy-style shorty-shorts and a camisole?

That would take the embarrassment of this already horrendously embarrassing situation to a brand new level.

She shook each limb experimentally, hoping to be able to dismiss him. But she couldn't help but wince when she shook her right arm.

"That hurts?" he said, watching her way too closely. "It's the one you fell on when you toppled the chair, isn't it? You've got a mark on your temple, too. Right here."

He touched her on the bruised flesh of her

temple. His touch was exquisite. Tempered, almost tender, despite the powerful energy in it.

Imagine a mere fingertip making her feel like that! Miles's touch never had.

It made the years of spinsterhood and devotion to her company, which she had recently sworn to, seem like they could use some second thought. It looked as if they might be unbearably lonely. Not to mention boring.

Not to mention, she might be missing something she had *never* experienced. She had a certain breathless awareness of Daniel—tickling along her every sense—after just a few moments with him, that she had never experienced before.

What if Miles had been right? What if there was something more? What if he'd done them both a favor?

After months of nursing her resentment against her former boyfriend, the thoughts felt like a betrayal—of herself! Daniel was looking at her way too closely, as if her sudden confusion and self-questioning were an open book to him. His finger still rested with exquisite tenderness on the bruised flesh of her temple. "Are you going to be all right on your own?"

CHAPTER THREE

FURIOUS WITH HERSELF, Trixie moved her temple away from his fingertip.

How unfair was that? That Daniel Riverton had stumbled upon the very question she had been secretly asking herself while outwardly declaring her contentment in her new life of independence?

But suddenly, the questions all seemed different. It wasn't just could she manage her own business and look after herself and her apartment and her nieces? It was, could she live without feeling the way his touch on her temple had made her feel?

He was talking about right now, Trixie reminded herself sternly.

Was she all right? The truth was Trixie was not all right. The unexpected twist her life had taken had made her feel rattled right down to her pale pink-painted toenails.

"I'm fine." This was said as much to herself, and her life plan, as it was to him.

Stubbornly, anxious to get her night and her life back under control, Trixie tried to get up from the chair, but pushed with that right arm. A startled gasp of pain left her lips. She sat back down, feeling horribly like she might faint.

He was on his knees beside her in an instant, his hand on her arm.

She closed her eyes against two kinds of pain. One, the pain swimming in her arm like a snacking shark, the other the pain of being so close to such a devastatingly attractive, nearly naked man in such horrible circumstances.

He prodded and tugged gently. "I think your arm might be broken," he said. "Or dislocated? Maybe at the shoulder."

"But my arm can't be broken! Or dislocated. I'm barely managing the twins now!" she wailed. The admission was out before she could stop it. Fresh tears pooled in her eyes, and he frowned at her, troubled.

"Where's your phone? Your arm is in bad shape, and you've had quite a knock on your head. I'm calling an ambulance."

"No."

"No?" His eyebrow shot upward in shocked surprise, as if no one had ever uttered that word to him. Which seemed like a distinct possibility.

"I mean you can't," she stammered, and then stronger. "I mean, I can't."

"Well, I can, and you are, so live with it. The phone, please?"

It penetrated the fog of her pain and her relief over being rescued that Daniel Riverton was a man just a little too accustomed to getting his own way. And as tempting as it was to have someone taking charge in a situation like this, she couldn't just give in. She had responsibilities!

"What about my nieces?"

His gaze shifted to Molly and Pauline. The next time she was thinking how attractive he was, she would remember *that* look. What kind of person looked at innocent children with such undisguised dislike?

Though, much as she hated to admit it, her own view of their innocence was slightly tempered now that they had tied her to a chair with near catastrophic results!

"I can't go in an ambulance," Trixie announced firmly. "What would happen to them?"

"Can't you call somebody to stay with them?" He was frowning at the girls, again, making no effort to hide the fact he found them faintly horrifying. She followed his gaze.

They had a jar of strawberry jam open and were scooping out the sticky red substance with their hands and licking it off. On her sofa. Which, while not new, was one of her nods to her new life, recently reupholstered in a bright, supermodern pattern of large orange and red poppies on a white backdrop, that try as she might, Trixie couldn't quite get used to.

Could she call somebody to stay with her nieces? It was obvious her arm was going to need medical attention.

Trixie contemplated calling Brianna. Her closest friend lived on the other side of the city, which was strike one. It would be at least forty-five minutes before she could be here. And Brianna would have to be at work in just a few hours, which was strike two. But strike three? Brianna had been nearly as horrified by the twins as Daniel Riverton was.

They are absolute terrors, Trix, she had said, part way through a play date with her own son, Peter. *How are you going to survive this?*

Apparently without any help from her friend, who had protectively installed Petie in his car seat and driven away well before the scheduled end of the play date.

"I'm afraid I haven't anyone to call," she said.

"Mrs. Bulittle?" he suggested helpfully.

She shuddered. "My twin sister, Abigail, would kill me if I left them with a stranger. I think she demands criminal record checks on everyone who is around her children."

"Amazing," he muttered, casting her a look that she interpreted as meaning *there are two of you, really?* But then he cast another glance at the jam-covered twins. "I think they could give the most hardened felon a run for his money."

She wanted to tell him that wasn't funny, but she just didn't have the energy, and it was close to true, anyway. Both she and Daniel watched as one of them—she was almost certain it was Molly—casually wiped a sticky hand on the sofa.

"Girls," she said, and then, when they didn't even glance her way, a little louder, "Girls! Could you move to the table with that?"

They both ignored her.

He looked at her. "Are they always like this? I mean they seem a little—"

He hesitated, lost for words.

"Precocious?" she suggested.

"Um—"

"Cheeky?"

"Um—"

"Spirited!"

"Right. Spirited. Like savages. When's the last time their hair was combed?"

It sounded so judgmental! She was feeling like a failure anyway, she didn't need him pointing out her inadequacies!

"They won't let me comb their hair," she said, hearing the defensiveness in her own voice. "Abby is on a horseback trip through the Canadian Rockies. I haven't been able to contact her to verify if it's true."

"If what's true?"

She lowered her voice. "They said only their d-a-d-d-y combs their hair." She spelled it because the mention of the word was enough to send both girls into fits.

"Like the our-mother-lets-us-do-this-all-the-time story, that one also doesn't exactly have a ring of truth to it."

"And you would be an expert on when children are telling the truth, because?"

"Because I am a man without illusions," he said comfortably. "I am a cynic about all things, and a ruthless judge of character as a result. The cute factor of small children has no sway over me. In fact, just the opposite."

He didn't like children! A wave of gratitude swept her. He was not, then, the perfect man, no matter how exquisite his finger on her temple had felt! Not even close!

"So," he continued smoothly, "you know how you can tell those two girls are lying to you, Miss Marsh?"

She glared at him, not giving him the satisfaction of answering.

"Their lips are moving."

"That seems unnecessarily harsh." She defended her nieces despite her horrible inner concession that he might well be right. "Besides, if you thought you had noise complaints before, Mr. Riverton, you should have heard Molly when I tried to take a brush to her hair. It sounded as if I was killing my cat."

It was the first time she had thought of her cat since this debacle started.

"Oh! My cat! The apartment door isn't open to the hallway, is it?"

He took a step back from her and craned his neck. "I think it is."

She had a sudden awful thought that Freddy might have slipped out the door in all the ruckus. He'd been unhappy since the arrival of the girls. How unhappy? Would he have taken advantage of the open door to explore a larger world? Find a new home?

"But I don't think you have to worry about your cat. He hightailed it down the hallway toward the bedrooms when I came in. I suspect he'll remain there for at least a month."

At the risk of seeming like an eccentric who was way too concerned about her cat—which, she thought sadly, she probably was—she said, as casually as she could, "I'll just go check on him."

But once again, her effort to get up caused her to gasp in pain.

Daniel Riverton, who had known her all of ten minutes, sighed with long suffering. "Don't move."

But I don't want you to see my bedroom! Those lace curtains apparently said *run* to men. But the words caught in her throat. She did need to know Freddy hadn't escaped.

She listened as Daniel went and shut the front door, then imagined him entering her bedroom. The whole time she'd been painting and hanging curtains Trixie had loved the safe, cozy feeling she was creating.

Home.

But ever since Miles had cast a jaundiced eye on it—as if her decorating style represented everything that was wrong with her—she hadn't liked it anymore.

Now she had new plans! The space would be a more accurate reflection of the new her: vibrant, cosmopolitan, the antithesis of dull.

She had even purchased the paint for this vision of the new her, but somehow she just never got around to it.

Understandable, she told herself. Life was beyond busy.

And yet, with Daniel Riverton prowling her premises, she had a sudden fervent wish she had gotten the redecoration of her bedroom done. She didn't want him to see it, as it was. In the world according to Miles, it said way too much about her.

Boring.

Trixie wished she didn't care what Daniel thought of her. Too late. She already did!

"The cat is under the bed," Daniel said, coming back into the room, "And just for the record, he's nasty, too. And he *really* looks like he stuck his paw in a socket."

She scanned his face to see if he had drawn any conclusions about her, and was relieved he seemed to have focused on the cat. So she would, too!

"He's a Persian." Trixie stuck her chin up defiantly in the face of the fact her whole life looked like a chaotic mess to Daniel Riverton, a man who radiated a certain aggravating calm, control. "He needs to be groomed. Unfortunately, he hasn't come out of hiding since the arrival of you know who."

"I do. I do know who. Speaking of which, where is their…um…hair groomer? D-a-d?"

"Australia. He and my sister are getting a d-i-v-o-r-c-e." Which, Trixie was fairly certain was at the heart of all the trouble with the twins.

The impending divorce of their parents, the disintegration of their world.

It seemed like the wrong time to plan a trip, which had made Trixie slightly suspicious. And although Abby had not said so, Trixie was fairly certain her level of excitement about her return home to Canada and her adventure in the Canadian Rockies might have involved a new beau, met over the internet.

"I feel like they've formed a little team, and they are taking on a world they feel quite angry with," she said. Why had she told him that? It fell solidly in the he-didn't-need-to-know department, especially since he had already declared himself a cynic who did not have any kind of soft spot for children.

But for some reason, Trixie wanted to convince him of the innate goodness of her nieces.

"A little team? They're like rampaging Vikings!"

There! That was a good lesson in confiding in him, or trying to coax the compassionate side of him to the surface. He didn't have one! His attractiveness, which had started as an eleven on a scale of one to ten, should be moving steadily downward.

It wasn't. Which made Trixie realize she was more superficial than she would have ever believed possible!

"But it is a good cautionary tale," he decided, cocking his head thoughtfully toward the twins. "Anybody contemplating matrimonial bliss should just have a look at this. People should really think about endings rather than beginnings."

She found that very cynical, but since it was precisely the attitude she hoped to adopt toward her life, she said firmly, "I agree, totally."

He regarded her for a minute, and that sinfully sexy half smile lifted a corner of his mouth again. "Somehow, I doubt that," he said.

She was flabbergasted by his arrogance. How could he possibly think he knew anything about her given both the shortness and the unusual circumstances of their meeting?

"And why would you doubt that?" She made sure her voice was very chilly.

"Because, Miss Marsh, everything from the color of your toenails, to the little—" he squinted at her, "—teddy bears frolicking across your housecoat tells me you are not cynical. Your devotion to your cat, the abundance of eyelet lace and lilac paint in your bedroom and your determination to believe the best of that pair of matched bookend fiends wrecking your sofa, tells me a great deal about you."

Oh! He *had* noticed the bedroom. And he hadn't liked it any better than Miles!

"I'm redoing my bedroom," she said. "I even have the paint. And a picture on my fridge door."

She glared at him, hoping he would take the hint and be quiet, but he did not take the hint at all.

"You are," Daniel Riverton declared with aggravating authority, as if she hadn't said one word about redoing her bedroom, "a little old-fashioned, somewhat innocent and extremely hopeful about the goodness of the world and your fellow man."

He shuddered slightly as if those qualities were reprehensible to him.

She knew she would regret him seeing her bedroom!

"You think I'm boring," she said.

"Boring?" he looked puzzled.

She rushed on. "You make me sound like a complete Pollyanna. I happen to be a totally independent woman."

"Ah, fiercely independent," he said, amused rather than convinced. "Let me guess. You've had a setback. A man, I would guess. You're disenchanted. You've put all your dreams of babies, a golden retriever, a cozy little house with a wading pool in that backyard, on hold. Temporarily."

Her mouth worked but not a single sound

came out. She was in shock. It was true. That was the world she dreamed of, the world of her childhood, the place she longed to go home to.

Her whole world had just been clinically dissected in so few words. Was he right? And she did still long for those things, though it felt like a weakness to want a life so desperately that clearly others saw as unexciting.

Miles had been right, though he had taken his sweet time arriving at the conclusion Daniel Riverton had reached in seconds.

Irritatingly, Daniel was right about almost all of it. No wonder he was so good at business. He could read people and situations with startling accuracy, if a rather ruthless lack of sensitivity.

But Trixie was determined he be wrong about the most important part of it. The temporarily part of it. At least she hoped he was wrong! No! She knew he was wrong!

"Not that any of that is of any interest to me," he decided before she could get her protest out. "We need to talk about getting you some medical attention." He winced as one of the twins used a jam-covered hand to smooth a curl out of her face.

"You know," Trixie said, wanting to reassert her independence, to make him question his overly confident judgments of her, "don't worry about it. If I need a trip to the doctor, I'll manage to get us all down to the car."

"Look, it's not *if,* and I seriously doubt you can drive anywhere."

He looked hard at her, hesitated, ran a hand through his hair. With the grim reluctance of a soldier volunteering for a tedious mission, he decided, "I'll drive you."

She planned to protest it wasn't necessary. Then she moved her arm a fraction of an inch and the pain was so monstrous, she gasped from it.

He nodded knowingly. "I'm afraid you need my help, like it or not."

"Not," she muttered.

"I have to go get a shirt," he said, looking down at himself as if he had just realized he was without one. "I'll pull my car around, and call you when I'm downstairs."

She had a sense of needing to get this situation under control—her control—immediately. "No."

Again, Daniel Riverton looked poleaxed, as if he had never heard the word no spoken to him. Or at least, Trixie suspected, not from female lips.

It gave her a certain grim satisfaction that she, who he considered to be utterly readable and utterly predictable, *boring,* in every way, had managed to surprise him.She enjoyed the sensation so much, that she said it again, even more firmly than the first time.

"No."

CHAPTER FOUR

DANIEL RIVERTON REGARDED Trixie Marsh with annoyance. He probably should have kept his observations about her to himself. Now, her back was up. She had something to prove.

He sighed. She had really picked the wrong time to make a point. And the wrong guy to make it with.

"No?" Daniel lifted his eyebrow at her. "No to my pulling the car around? Or the shirt?"

She blushed scarlet, which he had known she would.

Despite the bruise on her forehead, the total lack of makeup and the housecoat from a cartoon series, with that crackling halo of rich whiskey hair and those perfect delicate features, including sinfully full, almost pouty lips, there was no missing that Trixie Marsh was a very pretty girl.

There was also no missing that she was that wholesome girl-next-door type, with wholesome girl-next-door type dreams that made him exceedingly wary.

Her eyes, even wide with pain, were clear and astounding, a blue that made him think, again, of dark purple pansies, and those blue birds that people insisted on associating with happiness. Her eyes also whispered at a hint of something that made him as uncomfortable as wholesomeness.

Depth.

But she was not his type. Despite the claim— he had barely contained a snort of disbelief— that she, too, believed people should look at endings rather than beginnings—she was blushing at her close proximity to a man with no shirt on.

He could see she was natural and unpretentious and probably subscribed wholeheartedly to happily ever after, even if she didn't want to!

She was the type of woman who pampered her cat. She probably knew how to bake cookies and bread.

He had never—deliberately—gone out with a woman who showed any kind of domestic inclination.

Despite Trixie's claim that her bedroom was going to undergo a transformation, it suited her perfectly now with its delicate shade of lilac, and impractical whites and laces.

She was the naïve type, easily fooled by the lies that children told her.

She didn't look like she used much makeup, unlike his type, who used it expertly. And his type would never be caught dead in a housecoat with teddy bears on it.

Of course, his type wouldn't take on child care, either, particularly not child care for a handful like the two little hoodlums sitting over there on the couch spreading jam to kingdom come.

"No to the offer of you escorting me to the hospital, not to you putting a shirt on," she said, and her blush deepened—either because she had used the word escort—or because her gaze fell briefly to his chest. She seemed to remember she was drawing a line in the sand, and her expression became almost comically stern.

"Though of course you won't have to. Put a shirt on. Because, you may be right that I can't drive. But I can just call a cab. To get medical attention."

"Okay," he said, folding his arms over his chest, trying to hide his relief that those jam-covered little monkeys wouldn't be getting in his car, which was new, and had hand-stitched white leather seats that had never had so much as a drop of coffee on them. "Call one. I'll wait until it comes."

She frowned. "Though the twins have to have car seats. My sister would kill me if they didn't. Do cabs have car seats?"

"Do I look like the kind of man who would know if a cab provided car seats?" he asked. The women he dated also did not have children. Ever.

"No, you don't."

She managed to make that sound like an indictment.

"It seems to me, when your sister chose escape from her marauding children, she lost the right to dictate how emergencies would be handled."

"Mr. Riverton—"

"You can call me Daniel," he said, a way of letting her know that since they were going to be stuck with each other for a while, there was no sense being formal.

She hesitated for a moment, and then the resolve firmed in her eyes. "Well, then, Daniel, you can just leave. I can handle this."

Something about the way his name sounded on her lips made the back of his neck tickle just enough that he regretted taking down the slight barrier of formality that had existed between them.

Formality? He didn't even have a shirt on! Which was probably all the more reason to be formal! He realized he, who was known for his nearly ruthless ability to maintain focus under stress, was becoming distracted.

He also realized he was negotiating with a woman who had suffered a bump to the head, who was in pain, who was exhausted, and who had no hope of "handling" this! His own resolve firmed.

"Well, then, Trixie—" he ignored the shiver at the back of his neck when he said her name, "Enough is enough."

"Excuse me?" She looked mutinous, but he didn't care.

"Negotiations are over," he told her, inserting steel into a voice that had made men who had built empires quake. "Since we—" *we,* his mind noted, *as in for better or worse* "—we are in this together."

How had that most guarded against of phrases, *for better or worse*, slipped by his guard? His boyhood had been peppered with that awful phrase, his mother pursuing a dream that he had realized was unattainable. How is it possible she never had?

The last time he had actually spoken to her, she was at it again.

It's different with Phil. We're going to get married in June. I had this wonderful idea. In-

stead of a maid of honor, what if I had a man of honor? What if it was you?

What if it wasn't? He'd gone into hiding. And text-only mode. She didn't know, but the new cell phone number he'd given her? Just for her, so he could get through his day without having to sift through her bombardments to get to business items.

"Are you okay?" The mutinous expression on Trixie's face was replaced with one of genuine concern.

He glared at her. The injured party was asking him if he was okay?

"Since we don't know what to do with the demons if I call an ambulance, hand over your keys. Presumably your car has the junior demon seats in it?"

She scowled at him, the concern evaporated, thank God. He needed to just get the job done. Trixie Marsh was dead on her feet and her face was white with pain. He turned to the twins.

"You two—"

"Their names are Molly and Pauline."

"You two, Molly and Polly—"

"Their mother hates that," she offered.

He cast her a glance that clearly said he didn't care what their mother hated, and turned his attention back to the girls.

"Go and get that jam cleaned off of you."

They looked up from their feeding frenzy, paused.

"Right now." He made his voice deep and stern and no-nonsense.

To his relief, the twins scurried off, and moments later he heard water turn on. He turned his attention back to Trixie. Her mouth was hanging open with surprise. She snapped it shut when she saw him watching her.

"Beginner's luck," she said. "They don't generally listen that well."

"I'm used to being listened to. So, give me your keys. Your car is?"

He could tell she was considering proving he was not always listened to, but she knew her options were limited. With ill grace, she struggled to get off the chair. He put his hand on her uninjured elbow to help, but she shook him off with irritation.

In light of the shiver on the back of his neck when she had said his name, irritation was a good thing.

She managed to find her feet. She went and plucked her keys off a hook in the kitchen.

"It's the little red one."

Somehow he had already known. That the car would be little. And red. Eminently suitable for a woman with teddy bears on her housecoat and a lilac-painted bedroom and cute little pink toenails. Not a car the kind of women he liked drove: sporty, sleek, expensive.

Not one of whom had ever made the back of his neck tickle by saying his name!

"I'll go put on a shirt and bring the car around to the front door. Can you meet me as quickly as possible? Can you manage them?"

"Of course I can manage them," she said a little huffily.

"It's just that you haven't really, so far."

"Oh!"

Ah, the bliss of her irritation! He turned and went out the door before she used her good arm to find something to throw at him.

Trixie watched the door shut behind Daniel Riverton. Her heart was beating way too fast, and she was aware she was breathing in his lingering scent!

What was wrong with her? He was arrogant. Bossy. Take-charge. Too sure of himself.

Dreamy. He was absolutely dreamy.

"Stop it!" she told herself. She was just exceedingly vulnerable. He had rescued her from a precarious situation. It was probably natural to feel this ache of awareness. Her senses were heightened, her every nerve felt as if it was strung taut, tingling with sensitivity!

Firmly, she turned from the door and went down the hall to the bathroom. Her nieces had filled the sink, and were standing on the step stool she had gotten them so they could reach. There was water everywhere. On the floor and the mirror and the countertops. Somehow—impossible not to, really, with all that water—they had managed to get their hands fairly clean of the jam.

"Faces, too," Trixie said, and then dared look at her own reflection above their heads.

It was worse than she could have imagined. Her hair was standing on end with messiness and static. It had chunks of tissue and white fuzz in it.

Her housecoat—which she had chosen the fabric for and made herself in anticipation of the arrival of her nieces, hoping they would think it was fun—looked ridiculously juvenile.

"Done," Molly said, holding out her little pink palms for inspection.

"Good girls. Now go find some clothes to put on."

"It's night-time," Molly said. "I wear my pajamas at night-time."

"Hmm." But didn't sleep. She didn't want to bring her nieces into the crisp night air in pajamas. Calgary's proximity to the mountains made the evenings cool, especially when it was still early in the summer.

"It's a contest," Trixie told them. "See who can get dressed first. Shoes and socks, too!"

The girls were off, leaving her to contemplate the disaster of her own reflection.

It was her right arm that was hurt, so a little makeup was also out of the question. Worse, while she dreamed of changing to her most flattering pair of slacks and that yellow linen blouse, the one that made her hair look like flame, reality hit when she tried to shrug off the housecoat.

The pain tore through her shoulder. Even if she did manage to get it off, then what? Underneath the housecoat, she had on her summer pajamas, a pair of silky pink shorts and a matching cami.

She couldn't imagine how, with the injured limb, she could pull on a pair of slacks, let alone manage all the buttons of her yellow blouse!

So, the housecoat was staying, which severely limited her options for damage control in the making-a-good-impression department.

She picked the lint out of her hair, and ran a brush under water, managing to flatten it to her skull with her left hand, which she was not sure was an improvement.

Just as she was locating her medical card, her cell phone rang. At this time of night, she knew exactly who it was and knew he must have kept her number close at hand in the event that he needed to complain about the noise again.

"Your chariot awaits. I'll come up and help you."

Daniel Riverton's voice was deep and sure. She cast a sad look at her sad self as reflected to her in the mirror.

"No, I can manage," she insisted. "I'll meet you outside."

Feet in slippers, housecoat flapping, Trixie herded her nieces out of the apartment, trying to shush them as they waited for the elevator, for the benefit of her sleeping neighbors.

"But what do I get for getting dressed first?" Molly demanded loudly. "You said it was a contest."

"I know, but—"

"I want a prize," she shrieked, just as the elevator doors slid open.

Despite the fact she had told him she could manage, Daniel stood there. In a few minutes, he had transformed himself. He had on beautifully pressed buff-colored slacks, a white shirt that Trixie's fabric-educated eye saw was silk.

She felt even more disheveled than ever, but Daniel was not looking at her. His eyes had widened at her nieces.

The truth was she had been so focused on her own inadequacies, she had failed to notice what her nieces were wearing. Dressed—orders obeyed for once—had been a relief and therefore good enough!

Now, she saw the outfits they had chosen through his eyes: Molly in a pink tutu pulled over jungle patterned pedal pushers, Pauline in a dress that she had put on backward coupled with colorful rubber boots.

As he stepped out of the elevator, Molly threw herself on the floor, working up to a full meltdown. "I want a prize!"

Daniel's eyes met Trixie's. His comment about Trixie managing—*it's just that you haven't really, so far*—played over again inside her mind.

But to her amazement, instead of stepping back into the elevator, doing the smart thing and divesting himself of this mess, once and for all, he stepped out of the elevator and crouched down beside the shrieking child.

"How's ice cream sound?" he asked.

CHAPTER FIVE

MOLLY STOPPED MIDCATERWAUL, eyed Daniel Riverton with grave suspicion. "Really?"

"Sure." He straightened and winked at Trixie.

Winked. Of course, she had to remember the wink was saying, *See? This is how you handle small unruly children.*

"I try not to bribe them," she said, aware she sounded faintly sanctimonious.

"I think you should try whatever works."

And work it did. Molly got to her feet, and moved soundlessly into the elevator. Pauline stared adoringly at Daniel.

"Do I get ice cream, too?" she whispered.

"You didn't win!" Molly yelled from within the elevator. "I won. You're a baby. You don't even have your dress on right."

"Of course you get ice cream, too," Daniel said. "You get ice cream, too, because you have better manners than your sister."

Molly glared at him, but fell sulkily silent.

Pauline simpered. They all crowded into the elevator. Pauline threw her arms around Daniel's leg and held on hard.

"Hey," he shook his leg and gazed down at the tangled mane of hair with consternation. "What are you doing?"

Pauline remained stubbornly attached. "Hugging you."

"Well, don't." He shook his leg again.

"Why?" Her grip on his leg tightened.

"Because I don't want to be hugged." He shot Trixie a look. It was the first time she had seen his composure rattled, and it was terrible that she liked it. It wasn't fair, she supposed. He had rescued her. But she wasn't rescuing him. No, she was going to enjoy his discomfort immensely.

"You could try promising more i-c-e c-r-e-a-m," she said sweetly. "But if you do, of course, you'll have Molly attached to your leg, too. I'm not really sure there is enough ice cream in the world if you start bargaining."

He held her eyes and contemplated her words with a fierce scowl that made him, impossibly, even more attractive. He looked like a warrior, backed into a corner, weighing up his options.

She involuntarily shivered at the directness of his gaze, at the hint of pure power she saw there.

Then he looked down at the little figure who now had a death grip on his leg. He was a warrior, confronted with the thing he knew least how to deal with.

Softness. Vulnerability. Innocence.

"Would you let go of me?" he said. "I'm not the warm and fuzzy type, believe me."

Trixie studied the cast of his features: no, not the warm and fuzzy type. Determined, powerful, charismatic.

But was there a softer side to him? Crazy to contemplate it, as if it was a mystery that needed solving.

He shot Trixie a look, his arrogance mixed with just the faintest pleading. She couldn't help it. She smirked. "You're the expert on handling small children," she said.

"I never claimed to be any kind of expert on handling children!"

"You implied it. You know when they're lying. You preempted a tantrum. I got the feeling you thought if you were in charge, their hair would be dealt with immediately."

"You're being ridiculous. I would *never* put myself in a position where I was in charge of small children."

"But surely—" she knew this was way too personal, but she asked anyway, "you plan on having a family someday?"

His derisive snort was more than an answer.

But beneath the snort, she was almost certain she saw the faintest flinch.

"I wonder what has happened to you to make you so cynical about the thing most people treasure?"

"Ha!" he said, "I knew it! I knew, despite your claims, you want the little house, the baby and the golden retriever!"

She was aware that he was way too astute, but also that there was a possibility he had turned it back on her as a way to protect himself.

"That's what I thought I wanted, once—"

"Aha!"

"Because I had it as a child. And I wanted it very much again. But you are right. A man broke my dreams. You know how you guessed that a man had broken my dreams?"

He went very still.

"I'm going to guess there is a broken dream in you, too." It was way too personal, it was too much information about herself, even if he had already guessed it. And it was way out of line to make such an observation about a man who had not invited it. He was in her life by pure accident. He had done nothing but try to help.

He gave off an aura of supreme confidence and control.

And yet she had felt compelled to tell him she caught a glimpse of something else underneath.

Dumb. Oh, well, she was dumb around men. Plus, she had had a most difficult and exhausting week, capped off with tonight's events.

It had brought down the normal perimeters that would have dictated her conversation with him. She could take it back, apologize, but she didn't.

Instead, she played a waiting game with him.

He glared at her, held her gaze for some time, but then he broke first. He looked down at Pauline. "Two scoops of ice cream if you let me go."

Pauline let go instantly. His relief was short-lived. As Trixie had predicted, Molly was attached to his other leg.

"I want two scoops, too," she demanded.

"My God," he muttered, "they're terrorists."

Trixie couldn't help it. She started to laugh.

He glanced up at her. "Okay, okay. Whatever. Two scoops. Just let me go."

Satisfied, Molly unleashed him.

"Thank God," he said with soft, but heartfelt appreciation.

"You really are allergic to attachment," Trixie murmured, evilly delighting in his discomfort.

"Our acquaintance has really been much too brief for you to be analyzing me," he said stiffly. "But yes, you're right, I am allergic to attachment. Unlike you I did not have a happy childhood that I long for. Quite the opposite."

Then he looked annoyed that he had volunteered that much and even more annoyed when Molly ran over to the elevator buttons and hit every single one, so they had to stop on each floor on the way down.

Daniel tried not to stare at Trixie. She was beautiful, and the trip to the main floor of the apartment building took forever, thanks to Monster Number One hitting all the elevator buttons, which made Trixie smile. And then when he looked annoyed, giggle guiltily.

Her laughter was light and fresh and faintly, delightfully fiendish. She was relishing his discomfort!

It should put his guard way up. He didn't like it that she was seeing things others had *never* seen.

Most people saw what he chose to show them. Success. Polish. Power.

I'm going to guess there is a broken dream in you, too.

And then, he'd gone and confirmed it! It aggravated him, possibly because it touched him in a place that was not guarded. A place he had not known he had anymore or maybe not realized he had at all. A place that felt real.

For an astounding moment in that elevator, it felt as if Trixie Marsh had the power to rescue him, not as if he was rescuing her.

Rescuing him from what?

He had the perfect life! He had success and money beyond his wildest dreams. Women flocked around him, women a whole lot more sophisticated and savvy than her. He was the owner of an amazing company, and more importantly at the moment, a completely soundproof loft!

But for that one moment, with her laughter filling the small, confined space of the elevator, all of it—his successes and his love life and his loft—felt empty. As if his life had been a superficial accumulation of "stuff" and somehow he had entirely missed what was real!

And what that was, the elusive secret of it, felt as if it could be found in her laughter.

The elevator finally opened its doors on the main floor, and he bounded out like a man being chased by hounds.

Her car was parked at the curb.

He glanced back to see he had left her, with her disabled arm and slippered feet and flapping housecoat, to try and herd her nieces, who seemed to have broken in two separate directions.

Daniel took a deep, steadying breath, filled with the scent of blooming lilacs, and turned around. He went and scooped one up, and grabbed the other by the hand. He glanced at Trixie. She looked like she was going to start laughing again, but she very wisely bit her lip.

Somehow, still juggling the two girls, he managed to get the passenger side door open for her. And the two girls into the child car seats in the back, which were more complicated pieces of equipment than he could have imagined possible.

At the hospital, the emergency room was amazingly packed with people, despite the ungodliness of the hour.

With one little monster still in his arms, and the other attached to his hand, he settled Trixie in an available chair.

He was back in moments. "Go see that nurse over there. She's going to do some paperwork, and then they'll see you right away."

Trixie stared at him. "How'd you do that? I obviously should not be at the front of the line."

"I threatened to leave the children unsupervised to rampage through the place."

The truth was this was one of his skills: where other people perceived obstacles, Daniel looked for solutions. And he was not afraid to use all his expertise—and charm—to get what he wanted. The little girls—and his obvious ineptitude with them—had worked in his favor with the harried nurse. And as soon as he had seen that, he had played it to the max.

All of which, he was fairly certain Trixie would not approve of.

"Find some kids books," she said, as she headed for the counter. "They love stories."

Daniel, children still attached to him, went to a leaning stack of books on a coffee table. Monster One wanted down out of his arms to sort through them. Soon, they had both filled their arms with grubby looking books.

He found three empty chairs, side by side, but the girls scrambled onto his lap.

"You can sit here," he patted the chair on his left, "and you can sit here," he patted the chair on his right.

They ignored him, leaning comfortably back against his chest, clutching their books.

"This one first!"

"No, this one!" Monster One gave Monster Two a shove. Monster One was definitely the troublemaker. He reached into his shirt pocket, and found, thankfully, a pen. He put a little mark on the tip of her nose.

He saw Trixie, standing at the counter, giving him a worried look. He gave her a thumbs up sign, and chose a book, showed it to her to inspire confidence.

See? I know what I'm doing.

They were taking Trixie away. She was still casting worried looks back at him.

Probably figuring out she really didn't know him from Joe and she was entrusting Abby's children to him. As if anyone would steal them! He doubted if he could give them away, though he entertained the thought momentarily: a sign made out of cardboard around each of their necks.

Free children.

No wonder Trixie had been shooting him worried looks.

The children, however, were oblivious to his fantasies. The two children snuggled way too trustingly against him, and Daniel reluctantly flipped open the cover of a book. He wished he had a handkerchief so he didn't have to touch the pages. The book was distinctly germy looking. And this was a hospital. What if contagious people had touched it?

"Once upon a time," he read, trying to overcome his distaste for the condition of the book, "there was a little bunny named Jasper."

His distaste deepened, but both girls sighed

with contentment, and settled deeper into him. He paused for a moment. Could this be *his* life?

I'm going to guess there is a broken dream in you, too.

How old had he been the first time? Probably about the same age as these girls. His mother glowing with uncharacteristic happiness.

"Danny this is James. He's going to be your new daddy."

Joy, pure and simple. He was going to have a dad, like the other kids. He was going to go fishing and have somebody to take him to hockey practice, somebody who could tie his skates tightly enough, somebody who didn't just drop him off with a careless *have fun* and a blown kiss. Real kisses damaged the makeup.

The new daddy, hopefully, meant the days of being dragged into his mother's world—*How does this dress look, Danny? Do you like this shade of lipstick? Does Mommy look pretty?*—were behind him. Maybe the television would be turned to interesting things like baseball, instead of gushy stuff that made his mother dab at her eyes with a tissue.

Daniel shook off the memory, annoyed with himself. Years since he had thought of any of that.

Or was it? At some level, had he been thinking about it ever since his mother had announced she was doing it again? Were these trusting little monsters on his lap prodding memories closer to the surface?

"Jasper tried hard to be a good little bunny." He read stoically, hoping, no vowing, not to think about his mother's upcoming nuptials, or his lousy childhood.

"Dumtin wong?"

A faintly sticky hand touched his face. Daniel looked down at the twin without the dot on her nose. Her face was sweet and concerned.

She was going through a d-i-v-o-r-c-e. That seemed to make kids extra sensitive to the moods of the adults around them, almost telepathic. He should know.

Again he was surprised—and annoyed—to have thought of that, especially within seconds of vowing not to!

"No, Pauline, everything is fine."

She rewarded him for knowing which twin she was with a smile that made his heart feel tight. He went back to the story, so aware of the children on his lap, their warmth puddling against his chest, a scent he was not familiar with tickling his nostrils. The girls' trust in him was both undeserved and complete.

A dozen stories later, they both still seemed richly contented. He was congratulating himself that he had more of a gift with children than Trixie had given him credit for. He hadn't even mentioned ice cream, and their behavior was exemplary.

But of course the gods liked to laugh at such confidence.

"I have to go piddle."

He looked at the dot on her nose. Naturally it would be Monster Number One, Molly.

"Can't you wait?" he asked.

"Wait for what?"

Tomorrow came to mind. "Your aunt?" he said hopefully.   ,

"No, silly!"

Silly. Had he just been called silly by a four-year-old?

"Me, too," Monster Number Two decided.

He hoped *me, too* was for the *silly* part. But it wasn't. Monster Number Two wiggled. He put her off his lap as if she was on fire. And then did the same with Monster Number One.

His instant reaction was one of panic. Panic? For fun, he white water rafted and jumped out of airplanes! He handled business emergencies on a daily basis! He handled million dollar deals and had merged major companies. He had built his own company from humble beginnings into a force to be reckoned with.

He could not possibly be panicking because

a pair of four-year-olds had announced a need for the facilities!

Daniel forced himself to take a deep breath and contemplated the logistics of a challenge nothing in his life experience had prepared him for.

Monster Number One, free from his lap, tried to dash off, perhaps in search of the washroom for herself. His arm shot out and grabbed her while he thought.

Did he take them to the men's washroom? What if someone was using it? Did he go in the ladies' washroom? What if someone was using that? It seemed to him, he could be arrested whichever choice he made.

He could send the girls in the ladies' washroom and hover outside the door, couldn't he? Or maybe there was a gender neutral restroom somewhere. He'd seen family restrooms in restaurants. But then what? What if they needed help? What if they didn't come back out? There were a few less than stellar characters hanging out here in Emergency—he had noted them all when he chose where he was going to sit with the girls. What if one—like that one over there with his head in his hands, and no doubt a concealed knife in his pocket—was lying in wait in the bathroom?

He could feel sweat bead on his forehead at that new and terrifying possibility.

"Right now," Monster Number One warned him, her brows beetling down in a truly frightening way. "I have to go right now."

CHAPTER SIX

DANIEL WASN'T QUITE sure what *right now* meant, but it seemed rife with potential for an accident.

He did what any bachelor could be forgiven for doing. With one munchkin attached firmly to the fingers of each hand, he went in search of a nurse to charm with his smile.

The bathroom dilemma had been solved by a kindhearted nurse who took pity on him, despite her busy schedule. Dot announced she did not want to hear any more stories.

He considered this a blessing since he was not sure how much more talking bunnies, turtles and giraffes—or trusting warmth puddled against his chest—he could handle. His throat was dry and he felt like he needed a drink, and not soda either.

But since soda was all that was available from the machine, he brought the girls over and let them choose their own drinks. He had to lift them up to insert coins, they insisted on pressing the buttons themselves.

As if pressing a button was an exciting adventure.

Was this, then, why people chose to have children? Looking at the world through their eyes made the most mundane things fresh, somehow?

He shook off the thought. Every moment like that—pure enjoyment over the pressing of a button—was surely more than counterbalanced by piddle moments, not allowing hair combing moments, taking toilet paper hostages moments.

The girls discovered the waiting room toy box, but if he had an idea that he was going to sit and read an ancient *Reader's Digest* while they played, he was mistaken. Molly-with-the-dot-on-her-nose ordered him to play with them, and was obviously willing to indulge herself in one of those counterbalancing moments if he said no!

He settled down on the floor with them, not sure he wanted to be engrossed in a magazine with old knife-in-his-pocket so close to the girls anyway.

He cast a warning glance his way, but knife-in-his-pocket did not remove his head from his hands. With Daniel's standards about germiness on temporary hold, he helped the girls build a castle out of building blocks.

But suddenly the hair on the back of his neck rose. He turned to see old-knife-in-his-pocket staring past him.

He followed his gaze. Trixie had appeared and was standing somewhat woozily at the entrance to the waiting room, scanning with eyes that seemed to be going two separate directions.

The housecoat was now draped around her shoulders, obviously impossible to put back on now that her arm was stabilized in a sling.

The teddy bear housecoat had not even given him a hint what would be underneath it. She was wearing boy cut shorty-shorts and a camisole in a frothy color of pink that reminded him of spring blossoming peach trees.

Despite the fact she was tiny, the length of her legs looked silky and endless. He felt his mouth go drier than when he had read all those stories.

He scrambled to his feet, aware of other people—men people, particularly old-knife-in-his-pocket—staring at her with a certain lascivious interest.

Daniel was astounded by the level of protectiveness he felt. He stared old-knife-in-his-pocket down, and only when he had settled his head back in his hands did Daniel turn his full attention to Trixie.

She had a dreamy look on her face, and a funny little smile, that made the hair on the back of his neck stand up. It was the look of a woman who had seen a man playing on the floor with four-year-olds. The look of a woman jumping to all kinds of erroneous conclusions, probably deciding if he was a suitable candidate to father her children!

Which he wouldn't be!

Were his palms sweating? He didn't want her to misinterpret what he was about to do!

Keeping his own body like a wall between her and the interested perverts in the waiting room, Daniel wiped his hands on his slacks, held out the empty left arm of her housecoat and guided her good arm into it. Then he carefully reached around her, took the sides of the bulky garment and the belt and tied it tightly. It was a bit like a straitjacket. Which was perfect.

"There," he said, satisfied, taking a step back from her.

She didn't even seem to hear him. In fact, Trixie didn't seem to be reacting at all. He looked at her more closely, and realized how wrong he had been.

The dreamy look on her face didn't have a thing to do with him.

"Is that orange soda?" she asked, her eyes locked on the sticky can beside Molly. Every word was slurred, and her eyes seemed to be going in two different directions. "I'd kill for an orange soda right now."

He should have felt relieved.

Trixie was coveting an orange soda, not a father for her children. It was a yippee moment if he had ever had one.

And yet, what was that he felt? Strangely disappointed that the dreamy look on her face had not been for him? No, of course not!

Quickly, he went to the soda machine and got her a soda. She held it, in her left hand, and he realized with her right arm immobilized in the sling, she couldn't open it.

He took it back, cracked the tab, handed it back to her.

She took it with her good arm, lifted it, crashed it into her face and giggled. She found her mouth and took a swig, most of which dribbled down her chin.

"Feel drunk," she decided.

"Yeah, as if you've ever been drunk," he muttered.

"Have so. Grade Twelve. Someone spiked the punch at the prom."

"Oh! Drunk by accident."

"Kissed Davie Duke." Her eyes suddenly

seemed to focus. On his lips. She leaned toward him, sleepily.

For a moment, he felt frozen, as if he was caught in a spell. He stepped back quickly, then had to reach out and steady her when she lurched forward.

She catapulted into him, and gazed up at him.

"You're cute," she decided. "Better than Davie Duke. And *way* better than Miles."

He could tell by the way she said it, that Miles was behind the broken dreams.

"I've only ever kissed them. Davie Duke once. And Miles. Two people. That's probably not enough, is it?"

The way she was looking at his lips was faintly curious and faintly predatory.

This was getting scarier by the minute. Her warmth puddling against him was entirely different and far more dangerous than when the two little girls had been on his lap. It was even more dangerous than the piddle moment!

Those two little girls, at the moment, heading, unsupervised, past old-knife-in-his-pocket and toward the sliding doors. Beyond the doors, he could see dawn beginning to wash across the parking lot.

"One little taste," she decided, and his heart did this crazy tattoo inside his chest.

Was he thankful or disappointed when she

clarified what she meant, by shoving back from him slightly, and lifting the soda to her lips with her good arm.

Her lips were already stained orange, which made him very aware of how plump and appealing they were.

He was not kissing a woman impaired on painkillers. He was not kissing Trixie Marsh, period!

Quickly, he guided her to a chair, went and grabbed the twins before they got out into traffic. He planted them beside Trixie who was slouched in her chair swigging soda.

"Don't move," he ordered the three of them.

"Aye, aye, captain," Trixie slurred. She saluted him, and hit herself in the forehead with the soda tin.

Daniel went and consulted the nurse, keeping a watchful eye on all his charges. He had a brief talk with the doctor who had treated Trixie.

He got told what he had suspected. Trixie had been given a powerful painkiller so they could put her dislocated shoulder back in place. The doctor was also concerned about the bump on her head. She should be watched for symptoms of concussion. A photocopied list of instructions was thrust into his hands, and then the busy staff moved on.

It occurred to Daniel that he was being mistaken for Trixie's significant other, someone prepared to look after her.

He wanted to call the doctor back and set things straight. Then what? Would they admit her to the hospital if she had no one to go home with? What about Little Monster Number One and Little Monster Number Two?

Instead of calling the doctor back, Daniel looked down at the instructions that had been thrust into his unwilling hands. What was he going to do? Refuse to accept them?

He looked back at Trixie and the twins. Daniel felt a dread similar to what he had felt contemplating bathroom options for the girls.

Obviously, like it or not, he was *in* this thing. What was he going to do? Abandon her? She had already told him she had no one to call.

Trixie could not be left alone, in this condition, with two small and unruly children. His eyes drifted to the clock. The whole night had gone by.

In a couple of hours, he was supposed to be at work. He had important plans for the day. The Bentley deal was going down today. It represented months of preparation and hard work.

Daniel considered himself a hard-nosed businessman, who had his priorities straight. Basically, it was a game, that he loved to play and that he played well. Whoever made the most money, won. And he was always the winner.

He was a little startled that he still even knew there was a *right* thing. And that it actually felt like the only thing, the only choice.

Ignoring the signs about using his cell phone, he yanked it from his pocket. Wrong one. His mother had started texting early, Montreal was three hours ahead of Calgary. There were six voicemails from her. He deleted the entire conversation without reading it, ditto the voice mails.

Swamped today, he texted her. Talk soon.

That was a lie. He wasn't talking to her, real time, until after her June wedding was out of the way. What kind of man lied to his mother?

He cast a glance at Trixie. Not the kind she would approve of, something he was determined not to care about.

Daniel called his personal assistant Greta, who was a no-nonsense middle-aged organizational whiz, who produced the impossible as a matter of routine.

After apologizing for waking her, he said, his eyes on the woman who now was sporting a poorly applied circle of clown makeup orange around her mouth, "I won't be in today. You'll have to cancel Bentley."

The silence was shocked.

"And find me a nanny."

"A nanny?" Greta's silence was long, as if she was considering the possibility she was the victim of an April Fools' Day prank. "You're kidding, right?"

"Do I sound like a man who is kidding?" There was a tug on his trouser leg.

"You promised me ice cream!" He glared down, and identified Monster Number One, by the dot on her nose. She let go of him, but there was orange hand print on his trouser leg where her hand had been. Monster Number Two needed no encouragement to take up the chant.

Trixie found her feet and wobbled over. "Ice cream! That sounds good!"

He looked down into her face, tried to shake off the two children attached to his leg. He could not believe his always controlled life had taken such a bad turn.

"Is it morning?" Trixie asked, suddenly confused.

He nodded.

"Have we spent the whole night together?" Loudly. He was pretty sure Greta heard her. And the children before her.

His assistant was going to think he had spent the night with a woman with children! He was always the epitome of professionalism with his staff. Except for occasionally asking Greta to order flowers or make reservations, his personal life and his professional one did not mix.

"Hang on a sec," Daniel said into the phone. He lowered it and covered the mouthpiece with his hand. "We spent the night together. Not in the way that would usually mean."

She arched an eyebrow at him. It could have been quite sexy, if it weren't for the clown mouth.

"I want ice cream!" Molly yelled.

"I don't know about ice cream for breakfast," Trixie said, it momentarily piercing her drugged brain that she was supposed to be the responsible adult.

But the funny thing was that ice cream did sound good to Daniel. And even stranger. It felt oddly good to be out of control.

He couldn't remember the last time he had allowed spontaneity into his life.

"A nanny," he said into the phone.

"Wait! Don't hang up! Your mother—"

The one place that his professional life and personal one did mix, Greta the unfortunate intermediary between him and his determined mother.

He pretended he hadn't heard her, and clicked off.

He would be rescued soon. Greta would find

him a nanny. Until then, what was there to do except herd all his charges out the door and find a place that sold ice cream as dawn broke over the city?

Why was he doing this?

Helping a woman in distress, he realized, a bit unwillingly, came as naturally to him as breathing. He had picked up the pieces behind his mother his whole boyhood.

And, wisely, it had made him avoid any kind of neediness ever since!

CHAPTER SEVEN

"DID YOU EVER think about the expression *gob-smacked*?" Trixie asked Daniel Riverton.

It was a ridiculous question, she knew that. But whatever powerful pain medication she had been given seemed to have removed the filters from her mind that kept normal people from blurting out whatever they thought of!

Her thoughts were just popping out her mouth! Though with extreme effort, she was keeping some of them to herself.

Because the truth was the reason the expression *gobsmacked* had come to mind was that her Australian nieces used it when they were amazed by something.

And what could be more amazing than the fact that Daniel Riverton was at her dining room table eating ice cream with her and her twin nieces as dawn broke over the city?

She had managed, so far, not to tell him she found him incredibly, outrageously, *gobsmack-*

ingly gorgeous. The truth was the gorgeous factor was going up minute by minute, despite the fact he had marked Molly's nose with a dot, and called the twins Monsters One and Two to their faces.

They had clearly bonded with him over story books, orange soda and building blocks. What he didn't know was that Trixie had looked out the window of the hospital examination room to check on him—and seen her nieces making themselves at home on his lap.

She had seen him tap the chairs beside him, a hint that would be a better place for them to sit, and had seen her nieces nestle themselves more stubbornly against his chest.

The girls so obviously missed their daddy, and Trixie did not think she was reading too much into it. They were hungry for male attention, and they were not letting this heaven-sent opportunity to burrow into a broad chest pass them by!

It had been a tender scene: his awkwardness, their trust; his size, their tininess; his reluctance, their complete enthusiasm. The scene had upped his gorgeous factor by about three hundred per cent, as if Daniel Riverton's gorgeous factor needed a boost!

"Gobsmacked," she repeated, and he looked askance at her. What did it matter what she said? It was obviously all a dream that she was going to wake up from soon.

There was no way she was really sitting at her dining room table with her strangely silent nieces at six in the morning, with Daniel Riverton and a tub of fudge ripple ice cream melting between them. The white fluff coating the floor and drifting about anytime anyone stirred it with their feet added to the sense of being in a dream.

The ice cream explained the silence of her nieces, who were gorging themselves. It wasn't a proper breakfast, but it was a dream, so who cared? For some reason the nutritional value of the breakfast did not seem nearly as important as the root origins of *gobsmacked*.

Maybe this was the beginning of a whole new life. One in which Trixie was not overly responsible and totally predictable—*boring*—but one where she was spontaneous, and free-flowing, a Bohemian, who could happily eat ice cream for breakfast!

"I have to say," Daniel said, licking his spoon with unnecessary sexiness, "I never thought about the meaning of gobsmacked."

"First you'd have to define *gob*," she told him, aware she was being way too earnest. Maybe because even in her drugged state, she knew she had to focus on something beside his lips.

Really, there was something pathetic about being her age and only having kissed two men!

"What do you think gob means?" she asked, a trifle desperately. "Spit?"

Spit came from lips. Damn it!

He was looking at her, smiling. More focus on his lips.

"Spitsmacked," she mumbled, "It doesn't have quite the same ring to it, does it?"

"Hang on." He got out his phone, looked at it and frowned. Then he slid that phone back into his pocket and retrieved a different one.

"Two phones," she said. "I'm gobsmacked."

"One's a dedicated line." He tapped in something, squinted at the screen.

A dedicated line? Did that mean for one person only? She thought it did. The awful possibility that he had a girlfriend hit her.

Though, if the frown had been any indication, it was a relationship that wasn't going well! Wrong to be happy about that!

"Okay," he said, "according to the website, *Know-it-All*, gob is a British expression for mouth, which falls open when surprised, amazed or astonished, which you then cover with your hand, thereby smacking yourself in the gob."

"Well," Trixie said, "that took the fun right out of it."

"Didn't it? Alternatively," Daniel scrolled down with his thumb on his state-of-the-art phone, "it may date back to pirate days."

"Oh," she breathed. "Better."

Very easy to picture him as a pirate, with that silky dark hair and whiskers darkening his cheekbones, jaw and chin. She really wanted to touch those whiskers, to feel the abrasiveness of them beneath her fingertips.

It was a good thing, given her impulse control issues at the moment, that one hand was immobilized by a sling, and the other was trying to manage her ice cream bowl.

And then there was that devilish spark that burned bright in his sapphire eyes. She bit back the desire to tell him he looked like a rather attractive actor known for playing pirate roles. Better than that well-known actor.

Instead she forced herself to look away from him. She looked down at the remains of way too much ice cream melting in the bottom of her dish. The chocolate ripple was swirling into the vanilla, creating a new color entirely.

"That would look nice on a wall," she decided.

"Your ice cream?"

She looked up at him. "The color of my ice cream melting. It's kind of a rich mocha. I already bought paint, though. To redo my bedroom. Black."

"Black?" he asked, setting down his spoon.

"Well, dark, dark gray. Did you know the human eye can detect over two million shades of color?"

For instance, his pirate shaded eyes were sapphire and sea, specked with stormy sky and turquoise.

"You're going to paint your bedroom black?" This was said with a certain insulting disbelief.

"Yes," she said firmly. "Yes, I am. With white trim."

"Black walls?"

She nodded vigorously. "And gray bedding. Many shades."

"Fifty?" he suggested silkily.

She frowned at him. "What does that mean?"

"If you have to ask, you're not ready for a black bedroom."

"I am so!" And—here it was—"The pièce de résistance, a zebra skin on the floor!"

He raised an eyebrow, as if she had said something particularly naughty.

"Well, maybe not a *real* zebra skin," she said hastily, feeling a stunning heat rise in her at the thought of naughty things, a zebra skin, and him.

He didn't say anything. He seemed to take a sudden interest in his ice cream.

"And a pure white chaise lounge. With a great reading lamp."

He looked up at her, and a smile tickled around the sinful temptation of his mouth. "Now, that seems a little more in keeping."

She frowned. The *boring* element suited her?

"And the point of this makeover?" he asked softly.

"Just a change," she said. She could hear the defensiveness in her voice.

"It sounds like you're intent on erasing a memory."

"No! A bit of drama. A bit of chic. A more sophisticated, grown up look. A reflection of the *real* me."

He looked like he was going to laugh. She glared at him, and he managed not to.

Molly and Pauline, full of ice cream, got up from the table, toddled over to the sofa, curled up against each other like two puppies, and fell instantly to sleep.

"I was going to try and get them turned around today," she said wistfully, more than ready for a change in subject.

"Maybe today isn't the day to tackle it."

"They'll be up all night again. I have this neighbor downstairs who is complaining."

"I heard he's moving to a hotel."

"Really? Oh, Daniel! You shouldn't have to do that!"

"It's no big deal."

"Isn't it?"

"No."

"I think," she said, "I have to go to bed, too. I've never been so tired. I feel weak with it. Of course, I can't. The girls. The mess."

"Don't worry. I've got you."

He'd said that to her before, and even without drugs, it had felt so good. Now, it felt even better.

Suddenly, it all caught up with her. Exhausted, both physically, and from the effort of not blurting out every single thing that came through her head, Trixie felt a tear squeeze out her eye. She scrubbed at it furiously with her free fist, but another came and then another.

"What?" he asked. He came to her side, knelt beside her chair. "Hey, what's the matter?"

"You don't believe I'm going to paint my room black," she wailed.

"I don't think that's it. Out with it. The truth."

"Do you have a girlfriend?"

"That's what you're crying about?" He looked a little shaken by that possibility! Well, who could blame him?

"Of course not," she said hastily. "I just wondered. The dedicated phone line."

"No, the dedicated phone has nothing to do with a girlfriend. It's for my mother."

"Your mother? That is soooo nice."

"You have no idea," he said drily. "So, why the tears?"

"Just been alone with all of it for so long." She ordered herself to stop, but it was way too easy to confide in the kind of man who had a special phone line for his mother. Even so, she shouldn't tell him the truth. He was a virtual stranger. They had been cast together by circumstances, not by choice.

She could not possibly share confidences with Daniel Riverton! But before she could stop herself she was babbling, the floodgates open.

"I am trying to erase a memory," she admitted. "I lived here with my boyfriend, Miles. My parents died just after I graduated from high school. I wanted to go to university, but there was no money. Then my sister met this Australian guy and married him and moved there.

"I was working at Bernard Brothers. I started working there as a part-time job when I was in high school. I worked there for eight years. I loved my job! I've been sewing since I was a little kid. My mother taught me."

"Custom men's clothing? On Eighth Avenue?"

She nodded and then wailed, "I got fired! Can you believe it? He's the one who cheated, and I got fired!"

"Miles?" Daniel asked quietly.

She nodded, too vigorously. "Maxwell Bernard's son. We were engaged. He's the only boyfriend I ever had. I've been going out with him since I was eighteen." She was crying hard, now, and ordering herself to stop to no avail.

What had they given her in the emergency room? Truth serum?

Daniel had a hankie and dabbed at her face. "Hey, hey, it's okay!"

"No, it isn't okay! He found someone else. He said he didn't mean to. He got bored. I guess that means I was b-b-b-boring."

"Ah," Daniel said, "now the black bedroom is beginning to make a new kind of sense."

"It got very awkward at work. Not that he worked there. He was too good for that. But Max was going to be my father-in-law, and he was teaching me everything he knew, and then, just like that, everything changed. I should have had enough pride to quit before they let me go. Did you know saying you are letting a person go just means you're firing them?"

"That's just wrong. You had rights, you know."

"Oh, rights schmites! I have some pride! What was I going to do, beg for my job back?"

"Sue for wrongful dismissal?"

"They gave me a buyout package."

"To prevent you from suing," he said, annoyed.

"I'm not the suing type."

"I'm sure they were counting on that."

"Miles was more than fair. He insisted I have this place. That's how eager he was to get away from me. I'm getting on with my new life. I used my buyout package to start my business. It's going well. Really well. I can't keep up with the orders."

"That's good." A moment's hesitation, and then, softly, "He didn't deserve you."

"Boring," she said, sadly, "He was bored with me."

"Bastard."

"Thank you."

"You're welcome."

"I guess I am boring."

"Nonsense. You used *schmites* in a sentence. Hardly anyone is that interesting."

"Are you patronizing me?"

"I wouldn't dare."

"Boring and pathetic," she continued. She

gulped in a huge breath of air to make herself stop, but the dam had burst.

"I called him," she confessed. "All that pride in not begging for my job back? I made up for it with Miles. I'd call and cry. Beg him to reconsider. No pride, at all. I despise myself when I think of it."

"Don't do that. Despise yourself. It was just a mistake, that's all."

"Thank you," she said solemnly.

"You're welcome."

She sighed. "Finally, I decided to make orange juice."

"What?"

"Lemons!"

"What?"

"I meant lemons. I made lemons out of lemonade."

He was smiling, and it encouraged her. Maybe it was true. Maybe she really wasn't boring at all! The pathetic part she could probably do nothing about. Except she would never repeat that humiliating, begging-to-be-loved behavior again!

"No, wait, lemonade out of lemons. Anyway, I had this idea for a cat restraint system," she babbled through tears. "Have you ever tried to get a pill into a cat?"

"An experience I have missed."

"Well, depending on the cat, it isn't much fun. My Freddy was my inspiration. He got sick after Miles and I broke up. Cats are very sensitive to energy and mine was in the toilet. He had to go on pills, and I was a nervous wreck trying to get that pill into him every day by myself.

"So, I invented this thing, think of a slinky, only covered, like a built-in vacuum cleaner hose. You set the cat in the middle of it, like putting him in the hole of a doughnut. But then you lift up these padded metal coils around him before he even knows what you've done. It tightens on his neck. He can't move, but he's not being hurt, as if he's inside a nice sock. That's the padding floating around on the floor. The girls thought it was snow. I have to clean that up."

She stopped, embarrassed, disoriented.

Daniel reached up with his thumb and scraped a tear off her cheek before it fell.

"It's called Cat-in-the-Hat. I have too many orders," she said, sadly.

"That's a good problem to have."

"Is it? I was selling mostly word of mouth. Custom orders to cat owners, a few vet offices. And then a few more. It was all very exciting. Took my mind off contemplating all the ways I was boring. Making lemons out of lemonade.

No, wait. Lemonade out of lemons. And then I got an order from Pet Paradise."

"The big box pet store?"

She nodded gloomily. "Ten thousand units. I've got a hundred of them done. If I made a graph of my progress that would be pretty awful, wouldn't it? I'd have their order done in about thirty-six years, and three months. Give or take."

He was smiling. He reached out and tucked a strand of her hair behind her ear. "I really cannot imagine anyone thinking you were boring."

"Really?"

"Really."

She smiled through the tears. "Of course, you don't really know me. If you did, I am sure I would reveal my natural-born boringness to you. I mean I like to sew. That's my favorite thing in the whole world."

He looked amused, rather than convinced, and Trixie suddenly felt ridiculously driven to show him who she really was! It didn't make any sense, after going to such lengths to share the black bedroom concept with him! But now, she couldn't stop herself. The truth serum was hard at work!

"My idea of a good time is to sit at home and watch a movie. And not an action movie, either. My favorite? You'll hate this."

"Try me," he suggested.

"Those silly romantic comedies. My favorite of all time? An oldie, but a goodie? *When Harry Met Sally.* Boring, I know."

"Well, maybe not the restaurant scene," he said dryly.

Daniel Riverton had seen *When Harry Met Sally.* And apparently not hated it. She bit her tongue to prevent herself from declaring him her dream man.

"With a big bowl of popcorn. Extra butter."

His lips were twitching. "That doesn't seem *too* boring."

"Fun? I go to the pet store and play with kittens."

Was he biting back laughter?

"I've tried knitting as a close relation to sewing. I went through a phase." She didn't say *after my breakup* but hc was a smart guy. He probably guessed.

"Everyone I knew was presented with matching hats and scarves and mittens."

"That's handy in Calgary in the wintertime. I'm sure it was most appreciated."

Feeling encouraged by his input, Trixic lowered her voice and confessed the worst of it. "I once knitted Freddy a hat. And thought it was adorably cute. Little holes his ears stuck out of, pom-poms on the tie strings. That's the kind of person I am!"

"Freddy?"

"My cat."

"Ah, more cat-in-the-hat."

"So, there you have it," Trixie concluded forlornly. "After being ditched for being boring, I've tried to think of ways to be more exciting, and the best I could come up with was cat hats."

"Don't forget the black bedroom."

"Which I have failed to execute. Even though I have the paint."

Daniel seemed to gain control over his twitching lips. He regarded her solemnly.

"I think," he finally said softly, "If I got to know you?"

She waited, holding her breath.

"I'd be gobsmacked every single day."

She searched the clear ocean sapphire depths of his eyes for a lie, and found none. And he was a man who probably dated women who did exciting things. Her drugged mind insisted on adding *in bed and out*.

But still, she began to breathe again, and the air felt full of life and the potential for healing, and as if it sizzled with a thrilling and powerful mystery that she had only just begun to unravel.

CHAPTER EIGHT

DANIEL CONTEMPLATED THE SITUATION he found himself in.

It was ten o'clock in the morning, and Trixie's apartment was completely silent. Monster One and Monster Two had fallen asleep on the sofa, and with Trixie giving him grave, slurred instructions he had gotten them off the sofa—he hadn't missed her distressed look at the large jam blotch—and into to their beds, and tucked them in.

Trixie had thought they needed pajamas but he had nixed that as way out of both his comfort and skill levels. He had convinced her it wouldn't hurt them to sleep in their clothes, just this once.

Then, taking one look at Trixie's face, he had guided her into her room, turned back the sheets and, after just a moment's hesitation, slid her housecoat off her shoulders.

She had stood there, swaying and blinking, in her delectable little cami and shorts.

She was adorable.

And something more than adorable. He had felt a sudden insane desire to run his fingers through her crazy hair, touch his lips to her orange-stained ones.

He had sat her on the edge of the bed, scooped up her legs and shoved her under her blankets as quickly as was humanly possible without hurting her bad shoulder.

With her eyelet lace trimmed sheets tucked up to her chin, he'd realized he should have helped her wash her face. She was still sporting the orange soda ring around her mouth.

But it fell into the wouldn't hurt her department, and that, too, was way beyond both his skill and comfort level, especially given that wayward thought about touching his lips to hers.

Trixie was asleep in seconds, snoring a sweet drug-induced purr. He glanced around her bedroom. Despite a bit of fluff having found its way in here, everything was in place. The bed was centered on a good quality rug, old-fashioned and probably a family piece.

Above it was a framed needlepoint of two frolicking kittens and a ball of wool, that said, "A home without a cat is not a home." Daniel was going to guess she had done herself, possibly at about the same time she was trying to outrun her heartache by knitting mittens and scarves.

There were three pictures, in ornate frames, on her antique bedside table: the cat, Monster One and Monster Two.

A collection of slippers were lined up neatly, heels poking out from under the bed. Her dresser had a mirror above it, and held a single hairbrush. He could not see any earrings for the tiny piercings he had noticed in her ears.

He had a sneaking suspicion this bedroom was never going to be painted black. Or see any kind of shade of gray.

Why would he feel relieved about that? Feeling a bit like a spy, he beat a hasty exit from her private space and all it said about her.

Daniel retreated to the sofa. He suspected the loud, ultramodern upholstering was one of Trixie's attempts to outrun the *boring* label. He stretched out his legs and folded his arms over his belly, and thought about what he was doing here.

And the word *boring*.

It interested Daniel that money and power had afforded him the opportunities to do all kinds of things that would be considered exciting, maybe even wildly so. He had travelled the world, experienced the adrenalin rush of extreme sports, indulged in all the glamorous and exotic experiences money could buy.

And yet, the thought of eating popcorn—with extra butter—watching *When Harry Met Sally* had the oddest pull on him. So did visiting the pet store and looking at kittens.

And not alone, either, a voice inside him insisted on saying.

It was crazy! He deliberately did not have a life like that! He did not have a life that contained slippers and needlepoint, cats and kids.

To remind himself of the kind of life he had had, he picked *her* cell phone out of his pocket, scrolled quickly through the messages—We've decided to come to Calgary for the wedding to make it easier for you to be there—deleted them all, and shoved the cell back in his pocket.

He had never had that kind of life. His mother had not been a homemaker. Knitting and needlepoint and cookies had not been a part of their world.

Daniel, this is Kenneth. He's going to be your father.

Had he felt a glimmer of hope as his mother had introduced this next husband-to-be? Yes, he was pretty sure he had.

And maybe that was why simplicity and hominess of Trixie's life called to a place in him that he had not thought of for a long time. A place where he had hoped for that elusive thing called family.

"Stop it," he growled at himself.

Why did the simple things in Trixie's life seem oddly *real*?

What did that mean? That this world he had created—power and money and success—was somehow not real? Had he somehow missed everything that mattered?

"I am beyond exhaustion," he decided.

And it was time to get out of the strange enchantment he found himself in before it made it impossible for him to find his way back to his own world.

Without getting up, he found his other cell phone in his pocket and called the office. He was not unaware that he made the call like a warrior who found himself in a strange land confronting bewildering things touching his talisman. Greta's efficient voice had an immediate calming effect on him.

"What's up there?" he asked, *needing* to connect with his life.

Greta told him Mr. Bentley was not happy about the cancellation of their appointment on such short notice.

"Can you meet him tomorrow?"

Daniel tried to care. He *had* to care. He had

to get out of here and back to *that* world. Where his whole life would revolve around the Bentley deal, he would live it and breathe it and it would fill every hole within him. For a while. And then there would be a new deal.

Every hole within him? He didn't have any holes within him!

"How are you doing on the nanny thing?" he asked.

"Not well." She said it reluctantly.

"This is an emergency."

Greta said, with just a touch of very uncharacteristic defensiveness, "It's not as if there is an emergency nanny service out there. I assumed you would want the best."

"Correct."

"So, it's not as simple as you think. The most highly recommended agencies are not taking new clients. They have waiting lists. But even if they were, they have a vetting process. It takes weeks to get application approval. They don't just send out a nanny to anyone. I've had them email me the application."

"I don't have weeks. I need a nanny yesterday. And only for the next five days or so. See what you can do to circumvent their system."

"Okay." But she sounded, again uncharacteristically, doubtful.

He let it sink in. The nanny had been his

escape plan. His exit strategy. He had been counting on that like a stranded platoon leader relying on reinforcements.

He had to consider the possibility of no nanny. He felt a moment of something he couldn't quite identify. A tightness in his chest.

And then he did identify it.

Yup. Panic. A full-grown man quaking at the thought of the monsters waking up. Or was it at the thought of being gobsmacked by purple pansy eyes?

Wait, he told himself sternly. Daniel Riverton did not panic. He handled things. That's what he did. That's what he'd been doing since he was a tyke. Now, it was what he was known for. That was *his* world. Why would he panic over something as silly as a pair of girls who barely reached his knee?

Or another girl, who had worked really hard at not being boring and who had hair the color of whiskey aged in a sherry cask? And the cutest little circle of orange around her plump lips?

He gathered himself, thinking fast, making a plan.

"Unless you can find a nanny, I won't be meeting Bentley tomorrow. You know what? Just put him off until next week."

What? It occurred to him that a good use of his stellar planning abilities would be to figure out how to divest himself of this situation, instead of digging himself in deeper.

And abandon Trixie, arm in sling, messed up on painkillers, to deal with this? She could barely be responsible for herself right now. He thought of her talking so earnestly about the origins of gobsmacked, and smiled despite his predicament.

Somewhere in him was a man who still knew how to do the decent thing, and he was pleased by that, like a warrior who knew his way home, who didn't need his talisman at all.

Daniel looked at the mess floating around, cloudlike, on Trixie's apartment floor. Obviously, she was not going to be cleaning anything anytime soon, either.

He sought refuge in the plan, which began to click together with comforting familiarity inside his head.

"I need a cleaning crew."

What about cooking? How on earth was Trixie going to keep those two little monsters fed? Obviously she could not serve chocolate fudge ice cream for every meal.

"And can you call Simon, the chef at Champagne's, and tell him I need him to prepare a child-friendly menu for the next five days. Three meals a day. Plus snacks."

"For how many?"

He hesitated at Greta's question, then answered, feeling as if he was standing at the edge of a cliff and made the decision to jump.

"Um, for four. Two kids, under five, two adults."

Two adults. Ordering food for all of them felt like the ultimate commitment, like saying *I do.*

There was that unfamiliar panicky sensation again.

"Anything else?" Greta sounded bewildered.

"Maybe don't send up the first meal right away. Midafternoon."

Considering his original plan had been to extricate himself from this situation, he'd done quite enough damage for one day!

He fought down the panicky sensation. He could be here and not be here at the same time. He could set up his laptop on the table. He had his phone. All was good. It could be a world inside a world.

Besides, his mother would never find him here!

He was doing a good deed, like a Boy Scout. It didn't have to be life altering. It wasn't going to be life altering! He'd just keep an eye on things, so he didn't have to guiltily read in the paper about the perilous result of an injured woman being left alone to manage two children.

And not any children, either, he reminded

himself. Monsters. Monster One and Monster Two. What did he know about keeping monsters under control? Nothing. It could still make the papers.

Plan, he ordered himself.

"Greta, have a look on the internet and send over some highly rated kids' books. And the top ten kids' movies of all time." He hesitated. "And some romantic comedy."

"And will *that* be all?"

"See if you can find *When Harry Met Sally.* And a theater-style popcorn maker."

"And that's all?"

"Yes."

"Could we talk about your mother for a minute? She's desperate to speak to you. She says it's an emergency."

Funny, nothing about an emergency in her texts. She was just trying to wheedle her way by Greta.

"Whatever you do, do not let her know this phone number. Or that I'm at Kevin's apartment."

"But she lives in Montreal!"

"Ever heard of an airplane? She's within hours of striking."

This was greeted with silence that he was fairly certain was disapproving. He didn't care.

Daniel ended his call, contemplated the ceiling for a moment, and came up with a plan for himself.

Trixie was sleeping. The kids were sleeping. This would be an excellent time to go one floor down, and shave and change clothes. He could make some phone calls and organize his staff to function without him. He should probably call Bentley personally and apologize. He could gather up his computer, and the files he was working on.

It was the best of plans.

Instead, he kicked off his shoes and put his legs up on the sofa, found a cushion to support his neck. He fell asleep instantly.

Trixie woke up, startled. It felt as if her mouth was full of cotton, and her head felt like a team of demon elves were on the inside of it, pounding their way out. She rolled on her side to look at the clock, and gasped in pain. She rolled back and cast a look at her arm, wrapped in a blue sling.

Oh, boy. It was all starting to come back to her.

Her cat, Freddy, leaped off the bed, and a small cloud of white fluff scattered and floated up when he landed on the floor.

It was three o'clock in the afternoon. How could it be? She listened. The apartment was still and silent. She could only hope that meant Molly and Pauline were still sleeping, not stealthily applying their substantial destructive abilities to her walls, sofa, carpets or cat.

No, the cat had just been here, plus he would never be silent if they had him!

But, if they were still sleeping, it didn't bode well for keeping them quiet tonight—she really didn't want Daniel Riverton complaining about the noise anymore.

Daniel! He must have put her to bed—she certainly had no memory of getting here—and let himself out.

What she did have memories of, was sitting at her dining room table across from him, discussing semantics and decorating. Good grief, and confessing her life story! Including the demise of her relationship and knitting a hat for Freddy.

Including *begging* Miles to come back. She could feel the shame of doing that—and then confessing it to Daniel Riverton, of all people—burning up her cheeks.

"You never have to see him again," she told herself, firmly, aware of having to suppress just the littlest twinge of regret at that thought.

Despite her shame at her loss of control, Trixie realized she was starving. And then the logistics of her predicament hit her. The girls would no doubt be starving, too, when they woke up. How was she going to feed them?

Cereal, she thought. She could manage cereal. And milk.

The pounding started up again, and Trixie realized, surprised, it was outside her apartment, not just inside her head. Someone was at her door.

I'm probably being evicted, she guessed, then wondered if that was possible. She did own her condo. Could she be evicted?

She staggered to her feet, glanced down at herself. She couldn't go to the door like this! She was in a stained camisole. Her shorts had a blotch on them.

Mocha colored.

She had an uneasy memory of eating—make that gobbling—ice cream.

Her housecoat was in a heap on the floor. She picked it up, threw it around her shoulders like a cloak and lurched out the door, fluff flying as she went.

She stopped as she passed the living room.

Until now, except for her very sore limb, and her pounding head, she might have been able to convince herself it had all been a dream and, except for the ice cream part, not a very good one.

But, no, that was Daniel Riverton, fast asleep

on her sofa. Considering, just seconds ago, she had hoped never to see him again because of her drug-induced frenzy of confidences, she felt faintly—what?

She studied him—one arm thrown up over his head, shirt not tucked, and pulled up revealing just a touch of his belly, hair and slacks equally sleep rumpled, whiskers darkening the perfect plains of his cheekbones—and tried to discern what it was she felt.

There was no denying it.

Trixie felt a little shiver of tenderness toward the man on her sofa. Given her performance last night—from lying on the floor tied helplessly to a chair, to indulging in a chemically influenced blurting of personal problems—what she was feeling at this moment defied logic.

She felt happy that he was there.

"Dangerous," she chided herself. "That is a very dangerous way to feel."

CHAPTER NINE

"I'M COMING," TRIXIE SAID, startled out of her thoughts about her wayward and unwelcome emotional response to Daniel, by the insistent pounding on the door.

Trixie made it to the door, and threw it open and prepared to prostrate herself before Mrs. Bulittle rather than lose the one thing she had left, her home.

But it wasn't Mrs. Bulittle standing outside her door. Instead, two women stood there, in black dresses with white aprons, embroidery over the breast pocket that read Maid 4 U. One had a vacuum cleaner embraced in her solid arms, the other carried a large pouch over a sturdy shoulder. The pouch was bulging with cleaning supplies, some showing out the top.

Trixie assumed her eyes were wide, but so were theirs. Hadn't they ever seen a teddy bear housecoat before?

"I think you must have the wrong address,"

Trixie said sadly, "though I certainly wish you were coming here!"

One stepped back, looked at the number on her door, shook her head, and pushed right by Trixie. The other followed.

Wow! That was a first in her world: wishes coming true so quickly.

The first one stood, hands on hips, lips pursed, surveying the mess. She turned and said something to her companion in what might have been Russian.

Before Trixie, ever mindful of her cat, could get the door closed, a delivery boy got off the elevator.

"Wait! 602?"

She nodded dumbly and he thrust a bag, embossed with the name Champagne into her hands. Champagne was the only Calgary restaurant that had ever made Canada's top ten list, and certainly Trixie had never been there.

The bag was warm, with smells wafting from it that were sinfully delicious.

"Champagne does takeout?" she asked, bewildered.

"I just deliver. I don't ask questions." He grinned at her, looked past her to the fluff, disturbed by the entrance of the cleaning team, dancing above her floor, grinned again. "Wild night at the clown convention, right?"

He was gone before she could ask what *that* meant or point out *that* was a question. A vacuum cleaner roared to life, and she turned, clutching the bag possessively with her good arm, to see Daniel Riverton leaning in the doorjamb of her kitchen, grinning at her.

Given that upon awakening Trixie had hoped to never see him again, it was just wrong to notice that the man looked damnably sexy in the morning—not that it was morning.

He was leaning there, thumbs hooked casually in the pockets of rumpled, very expensive trousers, as if unperturbed to find himself in a strange place, surrounded by the roar of a vacuum, maids, white fluff floating up like an indoor blizzard.

Was it possible she could smell him? She was certain that his scent: clean and sleepy and sensual was tickling her nostrils and making her lean toward him.

Which made his smile deepen. But then she realized the smile on his face was not exactly a sexy grin. The grin of a man who knew all her secrets! No, not even quite that. More the same way the delivery boy had looked at her.

But her time to contemplate the look on his face was limited. The vacuum cleaner had woken the twins, and they exploded from their bedroom.

They woke up with all the energy of puppies, and after a quick roll in the fluff outside their bedroom door, they began to run in a joyous circle—living room, dining room, kitchen, hallway back to living room, shrieking with delight as their little feet kicked up clouds of stormy, snowy white.

Though the vacuum ran on, both maids stopped what they were doing, and looked at the girls, frowning disapproval at the disruption.

"Let's get out of here before the ladies decide to quit," Daniel said over the roar of the vacuum. He took the bag from her hands. "We can take this down to the park and let them do their job."

Trixie stared at him. He was taking over her life. The maids were here because of him! And the food.

He had the ability to make wishes come true which was very seducing. On the other hand, he knew all her secrets!

It was time to draw her line in the sand, to declare her independence, to politely thank him for everything he'd done and to show him the door.

On the other hand, she had been trying, ever since Miles had told her she was boring, to become more exciting. This was an opportunity!

But she couldn't exactly "get out of here" in a

stained cami and shorty-shorts, both items barely hidden by the housecoat cloaked around her!

What was she going to do now?

He seemed to realize her dilemma at about the same time as her.

"Do you need help getting dressed?"

They both paused to think about the implication of that. If she was not mistaken, they both blushed about the same shade of crimson.

"I could ask one of the ladies—"

"No," she said proudly. She would think of something.

The cat shot by her, and she closed the still-open door of her apartment with her foot, scooped up Freddy with her good arm, and went into the bathroom and locked the door.

She set down the cat, straightened and looked at herself in the mirror.

Daniel's smile this morning had had nothing to do with prying all her secrets from her.

No, she looked as if she had, indeed, had a wild time at the clown convention. Her crazy housecoat was draped over her shoulders like a cape, her hair was once again standing up like dandelion fluff, and her mouth had a huge, orange soda pop ring around it!

"What is *foie gras*, exactly?" Trixie asked.

Daniel watched as she sifted through the

bag of goodies from Champagne and solemnly studied the hand-printed calligraphy menu that had been provided with their lunch.

They were finally at the park, sitting on a thick, plaid blanket Trixie had found and spread on a lush carpet of green grass. Daniel did not know, in the chaos of getting ready to leave, how she could have remembered a picnic blanket!

He could not believe the effort it took to get two small girls ready to go anywhere.

"Even with both of us teamed up against them, it's like trying to herd gophers," he muttered.

"Not teamed up *against* them, exactly," Trixie protested, but weakly.

Finally the twins had been ready in fresh shorts and T-shirts—not identical at his insistence, since Molly's dot was fading—faces and hands washed, a bag packed full of juice boxes and moist towelettes and toys that included embarrassingly clothing-free dollies.

Their hair was not combed—since the very suggestion had led to screaming that drowned out the vacuum cleaner—but other than that, they looked cute and quite presentable.

Nevertheless the whole agonizingly slow process of getting out the door had made Daniel congratulate himself again on the wisdom of not having a family!

He wasn't quite sure how Trixie had gotten herself ready, though he was pretty sure it involved removing her arm from the sling temporarily—but Trixie was finally out of the silky shorts, cami and teddy bear housecoat.

She had put on capris and a sunshine-yellow buttoned blouse. The buttons had proved too much for her, and they were done up in the wrong holes, a fact that was almost disguised by the sling. He was going to pretend he hadn't noticed that, just as she was.

Her hair had been flattened with water, but now as it dried, it was springing free of her efforts to control it.

He was the only one who hadn't managed to freshen up, still unshaven and in the same clothes he had slept in.

Now they were sitting on the blanket, which he found quite uncomfortable, possibly because the twins, for some unfathomable reason, were sitting on either side of him, pushing against him in their efforts to get closer. Trixie, cross-legged, and looking like she didn't mind the absence of civilized furniture at all, was frowning at the menu.

"Quebec Moulard duck foie gras," she read. She dug through the bag and came out with four tiny individual clear plastic containers. She squinted at them suspiciously. "But what is it?"

"Hang on." He pulled out his business phone, caught a glimpse of a text message from Greta, that began Urgent, your mother...

He thumbed quickly to a different screen. "Oh, boy. You might not want to know what foie gras is."

"I'll try to be brave."

"Okay. It translates, literally, as fat liver. From a goose or duck that has been force fed with a gavage."

She looked a little pale as she set down the containers. "Okay, that's it for bravery for one day. And a gavage is? Never mind. I really don't want to know.

"I want that!" Molly, pretty-in-pink, decided. Quick as the gopher he'd declared she was earlier, Molly shot across the blanket, scooped up one container for her and one for her sister, and returned to his side.

Trixie hesitated, then handed Molly one of the provided spoons. Molly pried the lid off the container and ate the entire serving in one gulp. Pauline had the other lid off, and didn't bother with a spoon.

"Some of that is Daniel's," Trixie cried as Molly grabbed the remaining two containers, pried off the lids and disposed of the contents in about ten seconds flat.

"Don't worry," he said at Trixie's distressed expression. "Now that I know what it is, I'm not sure I'm man enough to eat it. Sorry, you didn't get any."

"It's quite all right. I said I was all done being brave for the day. I don't think I have a sophisticated enough palete for fat liver."

The contents of the rest of bag from Champagne was, thankfully, a huge hit: roast pheasant sandwiches cut into the shapes of turtles, fresh strawberries and grapes, chocolate mousse in individual cups. There was even a bottle of sparkling juice and four plastic wine glasses to drink it out of.

It wasn't until they were done eating, and the girls had run off to play on the playground equipment, that the distressed look returned to Trixie's face.

"What was that worth?" she asked. She was gazing at one of the spoons. "Who puts real spoons in takeout?"

"Don't worry about it."

"No. I *am* worried about it. I'll have to pay you back."

"You didn't even eat the fat liver."

"I'll have to pay you back, nonetheless."

"No, you don't."

"Yes, I do." Her chin tilted proudly. He had no idea what a bagged lunch from Champagne was worth, but he was willing to guess it was out of her price range.

He hadn't even thought of this. That Trixie would not accept it as a gift. Daniel was accustomed to giving gifts to women. Very expensive gifts. He thought, given who he was, most women expected it of him. Tickets to the best events. Fine wine. Flowers. Exquisite dining. Maybe as things progressed, a trinket: a gold locket, an emerald tennis bracelet, a diamond pendant.

He was accustomed to cooed appreciation. But he could tell from the stubborn cast of her mouth, that this was not going to go as expected.

"Can't you just accept it as a gift?"

"Absolutely not."

Not just no. Absolutely not, no. Well, that was about as far from cooed appreciation as you could get!

"We'll trade, if you insist," Daniel said easily. "You can give me some of those cat thingies you make."

"You don't have a cat."

"How do you know? Just because I said I'd never had the experience of giving a pill to a cat, doesn't mean I don't have one."

"You don't have one."

"Your certainty intrigues me."

"You just look like one of *those* guys."

That didn't sound very flattering! "What guys? The kind with no cat hair clinging to him?"

"Free of encumbrances, and intent on keeping it that way. Not only don't you have a cat, you don't have a living plant. I'd guess you can't even have a goldfish to keep alive."

He felt a little shiver at being read so accurately. The renovation plan for his loft had originally included an elaborate aquarium, but he had nixed that idea in a hurry. But really, being seen so clearly could be nothing but a *good* thing. Trixie Marsh was not the type of girl he would want developing expectations around him.

Because her kind of expectations he had already deduced, whether she would admit it or not, involved a cute little cottage in the suburbs, three children and a golden retriever. And a cat. Possibly two.

"So," Trixie asked, "why would you want to trade for cat-in-the-hats if you don't even have a cat?"

"Cute gifts?" he said.

"Please don't mask charity as a fair trade."

"It's not charity. I just did something nice for you. Is that so hard for you to accept?"

"Yes. I'm not the kind of girl that accepts expensive gifts from strangers."

"Look, it's not as if I met you after work in a pub and bought you a drink in hopes—" he wagged his eyebrows at her villainously. He hoped to lighten this conversation. He hoped she would laugh. She didn't.

She blushed. "I'm not that kind of girl, either."

He remembered she'd only had one boyfriend. Who had betrayed her. He saw the refusal of his gift in a new light. Trixie had no expectation of good things happening to her around men. It made him sad. It suddenly seemed imperative that he convince her to accept a nice lunch.

"There are no strings attached," he said. But even as he said it, he wondered about his motives. Because really, how was he going to get her to accept the nanny, if she couldn't even accept lunch? And if she didn't accept the nanny, who was going to help her?

Him?

"Besides," he purred, turning on the charm, now, "how could you think of me as a stranger? We spent the night together."

Her blush deepened.

"I know everything about you," he said. "I know you were engaged to a jerk named Miles, and you lost the job you loved because of him. I know you are going to make lemons out of lemonade." He hoped she'd smile at his deliberate direct misquote, but she didn't.

He rushed on. "I know all about Freddy, who inspired your company and you made a hat for."

Trixie still wasn't smiling. In fact, she looked appalled!

"I know you might have a bedroom with the walls painted black someday." Well, he doubted that, but no sense letting her know, so he added, "With a zebra skin rug."

He decided it might not be wise to mention she had declared him cute at one point, *better than Davie Duke,* whom she had kissed while drunk on spiked punch at the prom.

Why was he remembering every single thing she had told him?

Rather than look convinced that she should just accept whatever he offered as a gift between friends, Trixie looked like she was going to cry, confirming his wisdom in not mentioning Davie Duke.

"What?" he said. "Hey. Don't look like that."

"We don't know each other," she said, her voice trembling a bit. "You know way too much about me because you caught me at a bad moment."

"But I like what I found out about you!" he said, and realized, suddenly, that was completely sincere. "I like it that you used *schmites* in a sentence, and were curious about gobsmacked, and have this brilliant idea for restraining cats so people who actually own such beasts can get pills into them."

"The point is, while you were prying my secrets from me—"

"There was no prying involved!"

"Okay, I spilled my guts in a totally uncharacteristic and drug-induced state. You know everything about me. I know nothing about you."

"Oh."

"So, while I am not, apparently, a stranger to you, you are still a stranger to me."

That seemed unfair given how he had come to her rescue! Still, she wanted to know about him? Fine.

"I own a pretty successful company called River's Edge," he told her.

She snorted. "That's public knowledge. Give me that phone you love so much. I can find that on Goggle. It's not in the same league as *my boyfriend betrayed me, and I lost my job, and all I have left is my cat and I'm basically a total bore.*"

"Then I guess, I own thrce cars and a vintage motorcycle won't cut it?"

"Humph. Hiding behind your stuff."

Hiding? He flinched.

"Something drives you," she said softly.

I'm going to guess there is a broken dream in you, too. Daniel remembered she had said that last night *before* she was all ramped up on drugs.

He was *not* going to tell her.

"If I tell you, will you let me buy you lunch?" he heard himself say.

CHAPTER TEN

"MAYBE IF YOU tell me something highly sensitive about yourself," Trixie decided, tilting her head to one side, considering. "I'll let you buy me lunch. One lunch."

Don't tell her anything, he warned himself.

Daniel Riverton could feel his whole world shifting on its axis. Was he really nearly begging this girl to let him buy her lunch? Was he really going to exchange confidences with her for the honor?

"So, tell me one thing about you that no one knows."

He felt relieved. That could be just about anything.

"I have on plaid boxers," he said smoothly, and winked at her.

Other women he knew would have laughed. Other women he knew would have accepted this as an intimacy.

But Trixie looked faintly appalled and largely

disappointed in him. Why did he care? Why did her disappointment feel like an arrow going straight for his heart?

Because she had trusted him, doped up or not. Something in her had told her she could trust him and she had told him highly personal things about herself. Now, she had trusted him to tell her something back. And not about the color of his shorts, either.

He had a feeling, after the Miles fiasco, her trust in men was low, and that right now he could either restore it somewhat, or make it go lower still.

He was not the right person for this job! He was not the right person to convince her there was a man out there, somewhere, who was not a miserable self-centered cad, someone who was worthy of her dreams.

It seemed like this responsibility had come out of nowhere. And he was not prepared for it.

What about the rest of the food he'd ordered? He was going to have to call Greta and cancel the five days of Champagne meals.

What had he been thinking ordering all those meals? For four? He wasn't sticking around for five days! He wouldn't have a secret left!

"When I was in my first year of university?" he said.

Everything inside him screamed, *do not tell*

her this. He looked at Trixie. Something in her eyes called to him, told him it would be okay, told him he could trust her with it.

"I met a girl." *Shut up.* "We went out for two years. I loved her. I had never felt that way before."

In the distance, he watched the twins racing up the ladder of the slide, nearly on top of each other, sliding down squealing, Molly first, Pauline's legs scissored around her.

He didn't seem to be able to go on.

Trixie's hand crept into his. "Did she die?" she whispered.

He snorted and looked back at her. "It was a shipwreck, but it wasn't *Titanic*."

"*He* dies in *Titanic*."

Trixie was way too up on her romantic tragedy, where the reason for endings was death. Real life was so much less dramatic. He should take his hand out of hers. The warmth of her hand, the softness of it, the smallness of it, was like an enchantment. He was way too tired for this. His hand remained where it was.

"No, she didn't die." He ordered himself, again, to silence. He thought of stuffing the Champagne bag in his mouth to shut himself up. Instead, he felt Trixie's hand tighten on his, looked into the clear deep blue pansy-purple of her eyes.

He felt like a sailor who had been lost at sea, who had just glimpsed the strobe of a lighthouse piercing the fog, bringing hope where there had been despair.

Despair?

"She was pregnant." His voice sounded like a croak, as if he had run out of water on that lost boat at sea. "I wanted her to marry me."

"Then," Trixie said softly, "I cannot believe you are not married."

"Ah, well, this was in the days before I was as irresistible as I am now."

The joke fell flat.

"She actually thought my proposal was funny. She had way bigger plans than that. Way bigger plans than *me*. Being poor and pregnant and bound to a guy with no prospects wasn't part of it. She said she would have never married me, even if she wasn't pregnant. She had her sights set on marrying a doctor."

Trixie still had his hand. Her grip was surprisingly firm for such a small person. And reassuring.

It was like pulling into a harbor after being lost on that storm-tossed sea. He could trust her. He could tell her the rest.

That the girl who had jilted him thought, that while he was fun, he didn't exactly have a pedigree. He came from a poor single-parent family—his mother must have been in between marriages at the time. Her family expected her to marry what she had come from. Old rich. Stable. Ultratraditional. Her father, also a doctor, would kill her if he found out she was pregnant.

"So," he said, suddenly hating himself for telling Trixie as much as he had, biting back the rest, and grinning to hide the storm that had been stirred up inside of him, "There you have it. My secret. The place that drives me. Now can I buy you lunch?"

"What happened to the baby?" she whispered.

For a moment he felt as though he could not speak over the lump in his throat. When he finally did speak, he only just managed to choke it out. "She had an abortion."

"Oh, Daniel."

As if Trixie *knew* every single thing about him, including how soft his heart was. The way she was looking at him, he felt as if she could see him, lying on his bed crying, for the first time since he was a little boy, on the day that baby had been taken.

He needed to break the intensity. He withdrew his hand from Trixie's. "I run into her from time to time. At charity functions. She got her doctor." He smiled tightly. "I bet I make ten times what he makes."

Okay! Enough!

"Is that important to you?" Trixie asked softly.

He stopped himself from shouting, *yes,* and shrugged. "You know what she calls me? TOWGA—The One Who Got Away."

"And what do you call her?"

How had she known he called her anything? "NEMI—near miss."

She nodded, thinking about it. He thought if she said one smarmy sympathetic thing, he was off the hook. He could hate Trixie for pulling his secrets from him.

Instead she smiled. "I'll have to pay you back for the maid service, too."

He wasn't trading any more secrets!

Daniel, this is Martin. We're getting married!

He snapped that part of his mind firmly closed. "Look, it was my choice to order a maid service. Not yours."

"But I'm the beneficiary!"

"What you are is extremely aggravating." That wasn't really fair. He was aggravated with himself for confiding in her!

"What you are," Trixie said, snootily, "is just a little too used to having your own way! Some women might like that masterful approach, but I am not one of them!"

He'd already gotten that at her lack of knowledge about shades of gray!

"Luckily," he said, icily, "you are not one of my women."

"One of your women? What do you do? Keep a harem?"

It occurred to him they were arguing. And it occurred to him, amazingly, that he rather liked sparring with her. Her eyes were flashing and her hair was practically sizzling with ill temper. It seemed so much better than exchanging confidences. Safer.

If he was really going to use the masterful approach, he would kiss her into submission, à la Rhett Butler.

The thought of crushing her lips under his made him feel off-kilter. And out of control. What happened to safer? Well, that still seemed safer than exchanging secrets. If there was one thing Daniel Riverton never was, it was out of control!

"I need to make some phone calls," he said coolly. Cancel meals. Get on the nanny thing aggressively. Extricate himself from *this*.

But if accepting lunch from him hadn't gone over well with her, how was he going to get her to accept the nanny? They hadn't even worked out the maid thing, yet.

Molly-in-pink raced over and flung herself, uninvited, onto his lap. She grabbed his arm.

Her affection for him was as unexpected as him spilling his guts to Trixie. So was the warmth that welled up within him.

"Go play, now," he said, putting her off his lap. He gave his arm a shake, but Molly was clutching it like a homely girl afraid her date would get away. He one-handed his phone out of his shirt pocket.

"Can I have that?" Molly asked with a sweetness that did not fool him. She was already reaching. He held his phone up over his head.

"No, you cannot have this!"

"Can you come play with us?" Molly asked. Even if she didn't have on a pink outfit, he realized he was beginning to be able to tell her from her more subdued sister. That couldn't possibly be a good thing!

"I don't play with little kids," he said.

"Pleeeassssee?"

"No."

Pauline had been watching, standing a little off to the side. Now, she came over and plopped herself down, snuggling deep into his other side. "Dan-man not play, me not play," she decided. She cast him an uncomfortably admiring look with her soulful eyes.

"Tell them to go play," he said to Trixie. His

eyes went to her mouth. She had scrubbed the orange off so vigorously that her lips looked slightly swollen. A little crumb of something was clinging to the soft swell of her bottom one. "All this adoration is making me uncomfortable."

"You should be used to it," she said uncooperatively, "from all your women."

"Go play," he ordered the girls, curtly.

They wriggled closer to him.

Trixie smiled slightly. "You don't have to be threatened by it."

"I am not threatened by two four-year-olds," he lied.

"They just miss having a man around. That's why they've latched onto you. Their d-a-d-d-y loved to play with them."

Latched on seemed accurate. Now they both had death grips on his arms.

"Hell," he said, recognizing it as surrender. "How do you play with them?"

"Push the merry-go-round. Not too fast, though. We had an incident here."

"An incident?"

"They pushed it so fast my girlfriend's little boy threw up. Maybe start with the swings so soon after lunch."

Start, as if he had agreed to play with them. Which he hadn't. But he noticed he had put his phone back in his pocket. Maybe because Greta's first four texts all seemed to involve his mother.

"Is there anything likeable about children?" he asked. "It seems to me there is way too much bodily function and fluid, not to mention mayhem and noise."

Trixie actually looked at him as if she thought he was kidding, which he wasn't. That's what he got for sharing secrets with her! She looked like she didn't totally believe him.

She actually looked faintly wistful! "What's not to like about that?"

He got to his feet to escape the wistful look on her face, the sensuous puffiness of her slightly swollen lips. He got to his feet to escape the fact she was looking at him as if she knew something he did not know himself.

It whispered inside of him. He'd told her he wanted that baby. And he had. It felt like he had shared his deepest secret. Foolishly.

Aware he was losing ground, rather than gaining it, Daniel took a deep breath.

"Okay, monsters," he said, "to the swings."

CHAPTER ELEVEN

DANIEL WATCHED AS the twins, shrieking with noisy delight, ran ahead of him to the playground equipment. After a brief squabble, also ear-splitting, each claimed a swing.

He turned to see Trixie still on the blanket, trying awkwardly with her good arm to clean up the few crumbs of lunch that were left.

She sent him a haughty look that let him know that she was not amongst his adoring fans, and that she would never be part of a harem.

Or any kind of casual relationship.

No danger there, lady.

Still, he remembered the worried look when she had stopped to figure out what lunch was worth.

He wondered when the last time was that she had had some fun. Let loose. He wondered if it was ever.

It was none of his business. Who cared? First,

he'd let her pry his secrets from him, and now he was worried about her having fun? He was getting out of this situation as soon as was humanly possible.

Which meant he had nothing to lose, didn't it? She'd looked faintly worried ever since she had started considering the expense of lunch. Even when she'd been annoyed with him, she'd still looked worried.

"Come on," he called to Trixie. "You might as well come, too. I'll be careful of your arm."

She leaned back on her heels and folded her good arm over the one in the sling. "Are you trying to charm me?"

"If I was trying to charm you, you'd know," he said, annoyed. He was trying to be nice. How unfair she would try and see a motive in it! She wasn't his type!

But if she wasn't, why a renegade thought: how *would* he charm her? In the unlikely event that he was going to.

She was different than the women he usually saw. He had a feeling all his normal moves—the fabulous dinner, the expensive gifts, the tickets to the most sought after events, the glamour and the glitz—he had a feeling Trixie Marsh would see all those things for what they were.

A way to keep his distance, to avoid any true intimacy.

If he was going to woo her—which he most definitely was not—it would be kittens in pet stores, and bike rides along the path that bordered the Bow River. It would be movies and popcorn. And talks deep into the night. It would be fragile kisses, not crushing ones.

He blinked at the wayward path of his thoughts.

Trixie was still watching him, her position defensive.

"I don't know anything about swings," he said. "Or kids. I need your help."

She hesitated just a moment, looked down at the bag in her hands, and he could see her mental struggle.

Women did not struggle to decide whether or not to spend time with him! Then, still hesitant, she got up, put the bag in the nearest garbage container, and came over.

"You just get behind and push with the flat of your hands on their backs," she said earnestly, as if she really believed he needed her help figuring out the swings.

That was the problem with exchanging confidences. Now, she trusted him. She was taking him at face value. She didn't understand the whole flirting thing.

Of course she didn't! She'd only had one boyfriend.

Good God. Had he been flirting with her?

No, no, he reminded himself, only trying to be nice.

With his motives firmly reestablished, he got behind the twins and gave each one an experimental shove. They squealed their delight. "Not too high?"

"Are you kidding?" Trixie said, "The higher the better."

She was smiling. The little worry knot was melting from the center of her forehead. Mission accomplished. Good enough. Time to go home.

"Here, you get on a swing, too," he heard himself saying.

She gave him an uncertain look, then capitulated and took the last remaining swing. Daniel went behind her and gave her a strong push. Because she could only hold on with one arm, the swing twisted, and she gave a little shout of surprise and laughter.

When she laughed, it occurred to him, that's how you would woo a girl like her. Push her on a swing, until she was clinging to the chain with her one good arm, squealing with delight.

"Higher," Molly crowed. And then they were all yelling orders at him. They were all insatiable, with their cries for higher, higher.

But he had not expected Trixie to let loose quite so completely. Reserved at first, she was soon screaming right along with the girls. It was wearing him out, running from swing to swing.

He pushed their backs, and he found Trixie's quite lovely. Soft and supple. Still, it was wearing him out!

"Under duck," Molly commanded.

"Under ducks," the other two began to chant.

"What the hell, I mean heck, is an under duck?" he asked, panting. How could he be out of breath? His morning run was four miles!

"You push as high as you can, and then you run under the swing," Trixie explained.

"It sounds dangerous."

"We won't get hurt."

"I meant to me!"

"That's your incentive to run fast," Trixie told him, grinning. The worry was gone from her face and eyes completely. They danced with merriment. "Don't be a chicken."

The light she was radiating was making him decide whether or not to be a chicken. Call it quits on the game and get out of here before he was seduced into making it his life's mission to make that light come on in her.

"Bok, bok, bok," Trixie clucked at him.

Just a few more minutes, and *then* he'd figure out a way to leave all this behind him.

The monsters were crowing chicken noises

at him, now, too. A man could not leave a challenge like that unanswered!

"It's an under duck," he told them, taking advantage of the break to catch his breath, "not an under chicken. I expect quacking. The best quacker will get the first under duck."

They all began to quack, and he was able to catch his breath while pausing at each one and listening with grave attention.

"Quack, quack, quack," Trixie said with enthusiasm when he paused before her. He cocked his head, as if considering, and she did it again.

She seemed to realize what she was doing, and stopped, blushed, bit her lip.

"Your aunt definitely is the biggest quack," he decided, and watched as her embarrassment gave way to enjoyment. "Okay, explain this under duck thing to me again."

"Okay, come behind me. Don't push my back. Push, um, the seat. Kind of grab the edge of it, and push, and run forward at the same time. When it's high enough, you can duck right underneath it. Then let go and run like hell!"

"Auntie said a swear!" Molly said, clearly delighted at this transgression.

"It's not really a swear," Trixie said. "It's a place."

"Where people like me go," Daniel muttered,

to remind her—to remind himself—who he really was.

But he did as instructed. If pushing her back had been uncomfortable, his hands this close to the delectable curve of her seat was even worse.

But his suffering was rewarded with her shout of laughter.

He gave them under ducks until the park was ringing with their laughter. And his.

Finally, gasping for air, he could do it no longer. Daniel collapsed on the grass by the swings. He was aware of feeling sweetly alive. He could feel the sun kissing his upturned face, he was astonished that he could smell the scent of nearby lilac bushes mingling with the scents of petunias in concrete planters.

The little girls abandoned the swings, and attacked him. They climbed all over him, as if he was a piece of gym equipment. A ticklish piece of gym equipment. Stubby, determined fingers were crawling along his neck, poking his underarms, walking like spiders across his belly.

"Hey, stop it!"

But the more he tried to put them off, the more the twins shrieked their enjoyment at having taken him captive. He would pry Molly loose, and toss her away, and Polly would be upon him, pint-sized fingers seeking out tickle spots like heat seeking missiles seeking out warmth.

"Stop!" he yelled.

They chortled with fiendish merriment.

He finally managed to get them both off him at one time. The sense of the moment shining increased when he heard a sound, and looked over to see Trixie watching them, a light in her eyes and laughter running across her lips.

She looked carefree. He hadn't really noticed how ever present the worry furrow in her forehead was until the last twenty minutes or so had made it vanish. Her laughter was brighter than the sun.

He wondered what the hell—it was a place, not a swear—he had gotten himself into.

Trixie wondered what the hell—it was a place, not a swear—she had gotten herself into! She watched Daniel rolling on the ground, trying to get the twins off him.

"Come on, girls, leave him alone."

Naturally, as always, Molly and Pauline ignored her.

"There's ice cream at home."

That got their attention. With one final tickle each, the girls extricated themselves from Daniel and ran for where the car was parked.

Trixie watched him lie there for a moment,

like a man who had been knocked over by the percussion of a huge blast, shocked, disoriented.

And then he got slowly to his feet, glanced down at himself, and frowned. He brushed at his slacks, not that it helped much.

His face had a smudge of dirt on it, and grass clung to him. His hair was mussed, and his whiskers had thickened to a dangerously sexy dark shadow.

He was still in the same clothes he'd put on to go to the hospital, and they were looking worse for the wear. The Berlutis were scuffed and a coating of dust had taken their luster down a few shades.

"I thought you tried not to bribe them," he said, glancing up at her.

"I thought you told me to try whatever worked."

"Are you taking child-rearing advice from me?" he asked. "That would be just crazy."

But it wouldn't, really. The confession that he had very much wanted a baby once was changing the way she looked at him. But rather than admit that, she said, "It's been a just crazy time."

"Hasn't it?" he said softly.

For some reason her eyes fastened on his lips, and she could suddenly think of a way for it to get even crazier! She looked down.

"Those shoes were not made for under ducks!" Trixie said.

He glanced down, unconcerned, shrugged.

How was it, he looked even better than when those shoes had first appeared in her line of vision, when she had first gazed up, totally helpless, at her rescuer?

How could he look better than then, when he had been the best thing she had ever laid eyes on?

The truth was he seemed more real now, not the cover model for business magazines, but a flesh and blood man who laughed when tickled.

Plus, he had trusted her with a part of himself. He had given a secret into her keeping.

Was that why she had looked at his lips with longing? Because she knew something about him now that changed everything. It would change the way she looked at him forever. She shivered. Where was this going? If she just kept going along with it, where was she going to find herself?

She watched him scoop up the picnic blanket, shake it, fold it over his arm, and follow the girls to the car. She watched him lift each of the girls easily into their seats, managing the complexities of the car seats as if he'd been doing it forever, not as if last night had been his first time.

Daniel straightened, shut the door of the car, looked back at her, and this time she didn't look at his shoes. She held the intensity of his gaze, savored it.

Unprompted, the answer to the question, if she just kept going along with it, where was she going to find herself, blasted through her brain.

In love.

Now, that would be a hopeless situation.

And she was being utterly ridiculous. You did not fall in love with a man you had known less than twenty-four hours!

Their circumstances had been unusually intense. She had bonded to him because he had rescued her. And because he had ordered maids for her and provided lunch and been astounded that she thought she had to pay him back.

Because he had pushed swings and shouted with laughter and let the twins blow off some of that rambunctious energy and crawl all over him. He had tried, largely unsuccessfully, to mask his enjoyment as irritation.

And because he had told her about his college heartbreak. Without his saying it, she had known he had been devastated by the loss of the baby. He had wanted that child, desperately.

So, she had seen an unexpectedly tender side to him.

And then she had seen the man he would have been had his baby been born. He had a wonderful playful side when he had given her and the girls under ducks until he had them all shrieking with laughter, and then let them wrestle with him like a pair of playful young puppies.

Trixie reminded herself sternly that she had already managed—just barely—to survive a heartbreak. And that she was not setting herself up for another one.

Not, not, not!

Daniel held open the car door for her, and she slid in by him. His scent filled her nostrils and her senses.

She had to stop this. She had to stop it right now. For her own protection. This man was a heartbreak waiting to happen. She carefully rehearsed what she would say.

I can't thank you enough for your help. Don't know how I could have done it without you. But I'll be fine now. Couldn't possibly impose anymore.

But what if, instead of running from what she was feeling, she ran toward it? What if what she had seen and heard from Daniel was the truth about him? What if he was the man she had always dreamed about, and he held the key to the life she had always wanted.

The thoughts were absolutely terrifying.

As they pulled out of the park lot, Molly started to sing.

"If you're happy and you know it, clap your hands."

Pauline clapped.

"If you're happy and you know it, clap your hands."

They both clapped.

"If you're happy and you know it, and you're not afraid to show it, clap your hands."

Trixie tucked her hands under her thighs to keep from clapping them. Because, damn it all, she was terrified. And she was happy at the very same time!

Here was the truth of the matter: sitting on that blanket eating that crazy glamorous lunch, she'd been content. When Daniel had trusted her with a part of himself, she had felt a little stir of something more than contentment, a deep sense of being connected with another human being for the first time in so, so long.

And then on that swing, quacking like a fool, feeling the rush of movement and her belly tingling with each downward swoop, she had felt, for the first time in so long, the thrill of being fully and gloriously alive.

If you're happy and you know it...

She cast a glance out the corner of her eye at Daniel. He was looking in the rearview mirror at the twins, singing and clapping their hands.

"They are happy little gaffers, aren't they?"

No! They weren't. They hadn't really had a happy moment—unless you counted the one where they had wrapped her in toilet paper and tied her to the chair—since their mother had dropped them off and headed into the Rockies in pursuit of adventure and perhaps new love—all of which Trixie was convinced the kids knew at some intuitive level.

He was making them happy.

Could she really deprive them of these moments of relief from their angst over their collapsing world just to protect herself?

No. She was going to take one for the team!

Besides, as far as crushes went, it was a pretty safe one to have. She was the most ordinary of girls. Some would say boring. Actually, some *had* said boring!

She had had one boyfriend, and spent her whole working life kneeling at the feet of men like this one, completely invisible to them.

Trixie considered herself to be unremarkable in every way.

Except that he had said her hair looked like whiskey aged in a sherry cask. Except he had said if he spent any kind of time with her, he would be gobsmacked every single day.

But, really, that just proved the point that her crush was perfectly safe. He, no doubt, said things like that all the time, knew how to woo and charm, without investing a thing in it.

Daniel Riverton was like a movie star in comparison to her. While she had been leading her ultraordinary little life, he'd been on the cover of magazines. He was a millionaire many times over. He was accustomed to women flocking about him.

He was driven and ambitious and family was not even a low priority for him. It was a no priority.

His phone rang, and his brow furrowed, as he recognized the ring, and let it go.

"Are you going to get that?"

"No. I'm driving."

"Do you want me to get it?"

"No!"

Way too vehemently. A reminder he had all kinds of secrets. From the look on his face, as he ignored that ring, it was someone he did not want to talk to.

She was going to guess a woman that he did not want to talk to. Another near miss?

Trixie was reminded she was the type of woman Daniel Riverton would not have spared a second glance, if circumstances had not foisted her into his life.

Instead of feeling warned off, it occurred to her she could probably very safely enjoy the sensation of being alive that his presence brought. There was no danger of him returning the feeling.

For the benefit of her nieces—and to feel that again, that feeling of vibrating with joy and life force—Trixie decided she could suffer through a thoroughly unrequited crush.

Maybe, hopefully, the novelty would all wear off.

Since there was no chance of her crush being reciprocated, anyway, why not just be herself? After all, he'd already seen her at her less than stellar best: wrapped, head to toe, in toilet tissue; drugged up and talkative; hair scattered like dandelion fluff, and mouth circled in an attractive layer of orange soda; admitting she didn't know foie gras from fat liver and didn't want to either; clucking like a chicken and quacking like a duck.

Trixie freed her hands from under her thighs. "If you're happy and you know it," she joined in, "clap your hands."

And she did.

CHAPTER TWELVE

TRIXIE STOOD ON the threshold of her apartment, with her mouth hanging open, the key still in the door.

The apartment was silent and clean. The air smelled wonderfully of lemons and spice and all the things nice. The floors glowed. The walls sparkled. There wasn't a single piece of white fluff to be seen anywhere.

For some reason, for the first time since he had gone, it felt as if Miles had been cleaned right out of here.

The twins catapulted by her and ran down the hall to their bedroom. The cat shot out of that room as Trixie took her keys from the door.

"Get in," she said to Daniel, slamming the door behind him. The cat slunk into the coat closet.

"I think the cat has been vacuumed."

Daniel laughed.

She loved how his laughter swept Miles away

as much as the cleaning had. She loved making him laugh. She noticed even the door handle looked as if it had been polished. She wanted to clap her hands with happiness again!

In a daze, she moved into the kitchen. The sink and faucet shone. There were no fingerprints on the cabinets. On a hunch, she peeked in the fridge. Spotless.

Then she noticed a puffy, insulated bag from Champagne on the newly sanitized countertops. Scrumptious aromas wafted out of it, mingling with the smell of clean.

"I'm in heaven," Trixie whispered. But over her shoulder to Daniel, she said firmly, "I have to pay for that food."

Still in a daze, she went through the dining room. Her mail had been gathered and neatly stacked on the table. Beside that there was a box of brand new children's books, as well as two boxes of DVDs, one labeled Children's, one labeled *Best Romantic Comedies of the Century.*

In the living room toys had been sorted into baskets she had not had. She went over to her couch, and touched it.

The jam was gone. It was still faintly damp from being cleaned. Beside the couch was a popcorn maker like the ones she saw in theaters.

She turned and saw Daniel had come in behind her. He was smiling at the look on her face.

After their time at the park, he was sun-kissed and rumpled. His hair fell over his forehead. His shirt sleeves, casually rolled up at the cuff, showed off the toned, utterly masculine muscle of his forearms.

His smile was easy, and faintly mischievous, and engaging. He looked more like the boy-next-door than an influential businessman.

Her feeling of being in heaven intensified.

"I'm more indebted to you than ever," she said, so he wouldn't know what was happening inside her.

A realization was unfolding. That the novelty of all this—of being pampered, and being with him—wasn't going to wear off. She was just going to fall harder and harder and harder.

"I have ways to make you pay," he said, arching his dark brows and twirling the imaginary moustache of a villain with a maiden tied down to the railway tracks.

She thought the words were probably more true than he knew. She was probably going to pay and pay and pay.

And at the moment? She just didn't care. Enjoyment was for now, repercussions were for later.

"Why don't you see what we're having for

dinner?" she suggested, as if it was a given that he was staying.

He brought the bag from the kitchen counter in to the dining room table. She marveled at his easy familiarity with *her* place. How could he possibly feel so at home here?

While she watched, savoring each moment, Daniel opened the bag and peered inside.

Not even protesting the *we*.

Daniel took out the menu. "We're having charcuterie, spinach salad with Bosc pears and cranberries, grilled asparagus spears, lemon meringue pie with ginger snap crust for dessert."

The truth was it was a relief to not have to think about dinner. The truth was it was wonderful to have someone looking after everything. The truth was that she was in heaven. Absolutely and completely.

And Trixie had just enough instinct for self-preservation left, that she didn't want him to know that!

"What's *charcuterie?* I'm not sure if I'm up for any more weird foods today," she asked, loving it that she knew his phone would come out of his pocket, and his fingers would tap, and his brow would furrow in concentration.

"You didn't even try the *foie gras*," he reminded her. He looked down at his phone, read off it, "Charcuterie is a way of preparing food. It used to be a preservation technique before refrigeration, now it's used to enhance the flavor of meats, usually pork. Live dangerously," he said, when he glanced up to see her scrunching up her nose.

She closed her eyes. If this was living dangerously, and there was no doubt that it was, she wished she had started a lot sooner!

"Okay," she said. "But I'm in charge of dinner tomorrow."

Which assumed he would be here. She realized she was holding her breath, waiting to see what he would do.

"I hope it's hot dogs," he said.

"Me, too."

And then they were both laughing. And it felt easy and natural, as good to laugh with him as anything had ever felt in her whole life.

The apartment had always felt faintly stagnant, and now that was swept away.

Logically, Trixie knew she should at least be taking steps to ease Daniel out of her life. Logically, she knew the sooner she got rid of him, the less painful it would be for her.

On the other hand, it was also logical that she keep him around for as long as he was willing to stay! She told herself there was no way that she could deal with the twins with only one arm functioning.

She had barely been coping before! She had to humbly accept the help that was being offered as the godsend that it was. That was logical!

"Thank you, Mr. Spock," she muttered to herself.

"Huh? You're not a Trekkie, are you?"

"Not hard core."

"Wow, a girl Trekkie." He said it with reverence that made her laugh again.

And she knew, no matter what she told herself, the decisions she was making were not logical. There was no logic in a world made magic by laughter. There was no logic at all in the song of a heart.

And she realized she could not have walked away from the magic that was unfolding even if it had been the most logical thing in the world.

"Auntie," Molly called, "Pauline made a poop in the potty. Do you want to come see it?"

"No!"

"Dan-man?"

"Beam me up, Scottie," Daniel said, but he was laughing, again, too.

"Girls, wash your hands," Trixie ordered.

"Especially you, Polly," Daniel said in an undertone, and then they were laughing together, again.

For the first time in a long time, she did not feel alone.

She had not really realized that even with Miles, she had sometimes felt almost unbearably alone. For the first time since her breakup, she began to feel grateful that she had not married a man who did not make her feel like *this*.

As if the world was, indeed, a magic place, where anything could happen, where laughter could be the background music, where a hand brushing hers while pulling the contents of supper from a bag, could make her feel as if she was vibrating with the energy of the life force.

Later, they feasted on the contents of the Champagne bag, watched two kids' movies and tried out the popcorn maker. It was midnight when they finally managed to get the twins to bed, but even getting them to bed at that time was a triumph.

"I'm going home," he said. "To bed. I don't want to come in here in the morning, and find you wrapped in toilet paper."

It was her opportunity to tell him not to come in the morning. That she didn't need him. That, despite the arm, she was strong and independent.

But Trixie didn't say a single word.

In the morning, he knocked on the door, before she was completely ready for him, because the truth was, you could not be ready for a man like Daniel Riverton!

Still, her hair was behaving. She had clumsily applied a touch of lip gloss.

When she opened the door, his eyes went straight to her lips, which made the hardship of applying the lip gloss seem worthwhile.

He looked glorious in a pressed white linen shirt, and dove-gray slacks. He had shaved the pirate look away, but he looked as good clean shaven.

There was no Champagne bag, but he brought a bag of groceries for her: cereal and milk, bread and sandwich meat, hot dogs and buns.

When she asked, he gave her the bill without arguing, and he didn't argue when she went to her wallet, dumped the contents on the table, and one-handed, carefully counted out the money for him.

She knew it bothered him to take it. She appreciated that he had realized it bothered her more to accept it.

He helped her get the reluctant girls out of bed and fed. Despite the knife crease on those beautiful slacks, he got down on his hands and knees and gave her enthralled nieces horsey rides around the apartment to keep them entertained while she struggled to get herself dressed.

She wanted to put on a dress, but it seemed like it would be too telling a choice: *look at me. Find me attractive. Please.*

So, she struggled into a pair of plaid shorts and a matching tee instead.

"I've set up some movies for you. And I dug through the boxes and found some coloring books."

"Dan-man color with us?" Pauline asked persuasively, blinking at him.

"Sorry, honey, I have to go to work."

Maybe Trixie was reading way too much into it, but he sounded sad to be going. Or maybe she was reading her own feelings into it.

"Put me on speed dial," he said. "This is my private number."

In what world did Trixie Marsh have Daniel Riverton's private number on speed dial? She remembered that phone ringing yesterday, his choice not to answer, the look on his face. Probably quite a few people, poor souls, had that number!

"I'll be back to help out with lunch."

She knew she should tell him not to bother, but her strength and independence seemed to have been all used up getting herself dressed!

He arrived back at noon, made sandwiches,

watched the girls running around the apartment and announced they were going to the park to wear off some energy.

Once at the park, Trixie realized it hadn't been a spur-of-the-moment decision. He pulled water guns and water super blasters from his bag of tricks.

The war was on! They chased each other around the park, refilling at the fountain, until they were totally exhausted.

It was the happiest exhaustion Trixie had ever felt!

And when he didn't abandon her after the park, her happiness intensified. In the early evening, they went out on her balcony and roasted hot dogs on her barbecue, him taking the controls, and taking orders. Cooking perfect, golden brown hotdogs for her and the girls, then eating his own burned nearly black with great relish.

Daniel exprcrimented with roasting marshmallows over the heat, Trixie watched him lick the stickiness off his fingers with a kind of delicious hunger that was like nothing she had ever felt before.

Now, apparently, they had a routine. He arrived in the morning, left for work, came back for lunch and playtime at the park.

It was lunchtime and she heard his familiar knock on the door.

"Come in," she called.

Daniel walked into Trixie's apartment. When had he started to feel so at home here? Such a sense of comfort walking through the doors?

"Hey, how come this isn't locked?" he asked, sliding the door shut quickly. "Hi, Freddy."

The cat, still in the coat closet, hissed at him.

"I have a guard cat," she said lightly. "And in the unlikely event of an intruder, if the cat doesn't get him, the twins will."

"Seriously, you should lock the door." He felt a shiver of pure protectiveness. This area of town was odd, a very wealthy neighborhood bordered one that was not so up-and-coming.

For a moment, that feisty look flashed on her face and he thought she was going to insist on reminding him that she was an independent woman, and tell him to mind his own business.

Good advice.

Instead, she shrugged. "I just unlocked it a few minutes ago, knowing you would be here."

Knowing he would be here. "Hmm. I've become predictable."

He looked at her. She had an apron on over her shorts. She looked adorable, her face flushed from heat.

She was cooking something, like a newlywed waiting for her husband to come home.

Except that he didn't get to kiss her, the way a newlywed husband would kiss his wife. He should be feeling relieved about that.

But Daniel didn't feel relieved.

He felt a sense of loss. His eyes drifted to her lips and Trixie caught his gaze and went very still.

She stood, like a deer frozen in headlights, waiting to see what would happen next.

CHAPTER THIRTEEN

DANIEL LEANED TOWARD Trixie. Trixie leaned toward him. Molly—he knew it was her, even though she was not wearing pink and did not have a dot on her nose—exploded into the kitchen at a dead run, and threaded her way between them.

"Hello, Dan-man!" she shouted.

Pauline followed, stopped to give his legs a quick, robust hug, and then kept running.

The distraction of the children was enough to make him pull back from Trixie. She turned quickly away from him, her cheeks suddenly on fire.

"What's that awesome smell?" he asked, unsettled by his awareness of her, unsettled by the fact he *wanted* to kiss her and had wanted to for days.

Trixie turned and removed a sheet of cookies from the oven. They were golden brown, studded with melting chocolate chips.

"You can make cookies?" Daniel felt his mouth watering.

She shot him an incredulous look. "Everyone can make cookies."

"I can't. And you can do it one-handed?"

"The girls did all the measuring and pouring and stirring. They loved it."

He reached for a cookie. She tapped his hand with a wooden spoon, but he just laughed and snatched it anyway. Her kitchen was so tiny. With the two of them in here, it felt full. He could smell the fresh-from-the-oven cookies and a scent that was just hers: clean and pure as the earth after a thunderstorm.

"No cookies before lunch."

"I was becoming way too predictable," he said. "I'm going to live dangerously."

He popped the whole cookie in his mouth, aware he was not moving away from her. His senses felt amazingly heightened as the cookie melted on his tongue. "I think," he proclaimed thoughtfully, "that's the best thing I have ever tasted."

Trixie looked pleased, but her tone was skeptical. "Better than Quebec Moulard duck foie gras from Champagne?"

"If you recall, I never got any of that."

"Okay, better than lemon meringue pie on a ginger snap crust?"

"Way better." He dodged the wooden spoon, reached by her and snagged another cookie. "You missed me. Didn't you ever play that game at the fair? Smack the mole coming out of the hole?"

"I missed you on purpose. I'm trying to make a point, not hurt you."

He snaked by her again, got another cookie. "Hurt me?" He shoved the whole cookie in his mouth. "This is a cookie worth dying for!"

"Stop it!" She was giggling, and trying to look stern. It was a very amusing combination, so he reached by her again and grabbed two more cookies. She managed to land a light tap with the spoon that time. "You're acting like you've never had a homemade cookie before."

"You're right. I haven't."

She stared at him. Her eyes were huge, that drooping pansy blue that was so enchanting. Did she have a touch of mascara on today? "You have so."

"No, seriously, I haven't."

"How is that even possible?"

"My mother was not exactly the cookie baking sort of mother." Funny, how that felt: as if he was revealing a way bigger secret than he had the day he had told her about his college love gone so very wrong. He covered his discomfort with more cookie thievery.

"You must have had plenty of women try to win your heart with cookies!"

"Is that what you're trying to do?"

"No! My mother used to bake with me. And so I wanted to do it with the girls."

"I can honestly say, I've never gone out with a woman who made cookies."

Until now. Not that he was going out with Trixie.

"Well," she said, and looked hurt, "you know. Us boring ones. Baking cookies. Sewing up a storm. The excitement never stops."

"I didn't mean it like that."

"It's okay."

But it wasn't okay. He reached out and touched her hair, and she went very still. He leaned into her and this time he didn't stop. Without making a conscious decision to do so, he took her lips with his.

And tasted her.

Her taste, like the cookies, was something he had never had before. There was a purity about her, and an innocence.

And a hint of fire.

She parted her lips, and took the kiss deeper.

He heard the twins rampaging toward them again, and pulled away from her. He felt stunned.

He had been in intimate situations with

women dozens of times. Maybe even hundreds. Why was it, standing here fully clothed, he felt suddenly naked?

"Are you sure you're not trying to win my heart with cookies?" he said, huskily.

"Boring, me?" she asked, arching an eyebrow at him.

"There was nothing boring about that," he said, scraping a hand through his hair. How was it possible that Trixie looked taken aback and thrilled at the same time? He just caught her smile before the twins interrupted their game.

They were upon him, and he had to pick up each and toss them in the air in greeting.

That kiss had changed everything. It felt as if the very air was charged between them. Trixie could not look at him without a shiver of remembrance about how his lips had tasted.

She had only really ever kissed Miles. Davie Duke did not count because it had only been once and she'd been drunk.

Nothing about kissing Miles had prepared her for kissing Daniel. It was like a spark had leapt to life within her.

But he seemed anxious to pretend it had never happened.

Tonight, out on her deck, ready to barbecue, Daniel presented them each with a gift.

She was going to protest it was enough gifts, until she saw what it was. He had given Molly and Polly and her each a bubble wand.

As he grilled burgers, they sat on her deck enveloped in the delicious smoky smells. Long after they had eaten the burgers, as evening fell, they took turns blowing bubbles down onto the city below, watching in wonder as the iridescent orbs—some purple, some pink, some blue, some gold—floated endlessly up on the warm summer air.

When Trixie felt it couldn't get more magical, Daniel instigated contests. Who could blow the biggest bubble? Who could blow the most bubbles? Whose bubble would last the longest without bursting?

Pauline put her mouth too close to the wand. She sucked in, instead of breathing out. For the next few minutes, every time she spoke, bubbles came out her mouth.

Trixie was not sure she had ever laughed so hard, ever felt so joyous, ever been so engaged in the moment, and another person. She looked at him. Daniel was bent over from laughing so hard.

He helped her get the girls to bed, and then looked at her face.

"What's wrong?" he asked her.

"Nothing." Unless you counted the sudden realization that you wanted something you probably could never have!

"I can tell by looking at you, something is the matter."

When had this happened? When had they come to know each other so well, in such a short time, that they could read each other so easily?

She'd been with Miles since high school and he had never shown any real sensitivity to her. If she was crying, he might be able to tell something was wrong, otherwise, he was lost in the current episode of reality TV.

It occurred to her that maybe, just maybe, it had been Miles who was boring.

"Are you going to tell me what's bothering you?"

She did the only thing she could think of. She lied.

"Daniel, I haven't made a single cat-in-the-hat for days. I am so behind I'm never going to catch up."

"Let's make some right now."

She stared at him. "Seriously?"

"Sure. I'd like to see what's involved in putting together this contraption."

She scanned his face. He really was interested. He really wanted to help her. It just made that other feeling—of wanting something she couldn't have—so much more intense.

So, she folded her arms over her chest. "What's your hourly rate?"

He laughed. "You can't afford me. But you've insisted on buying all the groceries I've been eating, so I owe you now. Put me to work! I must earn my keep. I'll work off all the cookies I ate. Maybe I'll even end up with a credit, and you'll have to make me more."

He did that fiendish thing she was beginning to love with his eyebrows.

That was the problem! She was beginning to love so much about him. Up to and including the taste of his lips!

She had to send him home. But she didn't. She gave in with nary a fight and led him to her workroom. Her rough assembly line was really set up for only one person, so they were shoulder to shoulder in the tiny room.

"I've already cut and sewed the fabric, so today is just inserting coils and stuffing."

She chose one of her fabric frames, an adorable pink flannel with cartoon cats chasing mice. "I'll show you with this one."

He watched carefully, and then looked at her stack of prepared fabric. "Is each one different?"

"Absolutely. Pick whichever one you want."

Soon they were stuffing and assembling and laughing together. Conversation was so easy with him. He asked lots of questions about her company.

"Your questions are making me realize I'm a disaster at business," she said, smiling at him, and plucking some stuffing from his hair.

"You have to think of a business as a three-legged stool," he said. "One leg is your product, which is obviously excellent. Another leg is marketing, which given that you have more orders than you can fill, is obviously good. But the other leg is business: financing, manufacturing, your business model, your projections, your costs per unit."

"Leg three is where I'm falling down," she said.

"I can help you with it."

"Really?" Up until now, she had been aware of a clock ticking. She needed help with the twins, he would be here. But once they were gone? Would he still be here?

Was he opening this door on purpose? So that he would have an excuse to still be here once the twins were gone?

She stared at him. He seemed to realize what he had done. That kiss over the cookies was suddenly between them. He stared back at her. He moved one step toward her, and then stopped, considering.

Considering, as she was, how complicated it could all get?

"I mean, I don't have to personally help you," he said quickly. "I have access to all kinds of experts." He looked at his watch. "I have to go."

So, there was her answer. While she was falling deeper and deeper, he was looking for the exit.

So, it would be really dumb to give in to the desire to taste him one more time. It would probably scare him away for good!

But something about the way he was looking at her told her maybe, even as he wanted out, he was already in.

She closed the distance between them, and looked up at him. She reached up, and used another piece of fluff clinging to his glossy locks as an excuse to touch him. When she had plucked it from his hair, her hand lingered and she touched the now oh-so-familiar plains of his beautiful face. She had a feeling of being a passenger aboard a runaway train.

Somewhere there was an emergency cord to pull the brakes. But there was something about the building speed and intensity that was as thrilling as it was frightening.

She stood up on her tiptoes and took his lips.

That brush of the lips over cookies had been a prelude to this, a hint of what he held for her: her heart knew him. It was homecoming. It was the cooling rain after the intensity of the storm.

It was the out-of-control train gliding to a stop, a suspended-in-time moment of utter connection, joy, bliss.

He pulled her in close to him, explored the hollow of her mouth, while his fingertips traced her earlobes and eyelids and cheekbones and the hollow of her throat and the back of her neck.

And then, he pulled away from her, stared at her, stunned. Wordlessly, he turned from her, and bolted for the door.

When the door shut behind him, she was not sure she would ever see him again.

Trixie looked back at the work they had done. Daniel had made three cat-in-the-hats. They were all terrible. Unevenly stuffed, lopsided, collapsing. He had made cute fabric choices, which surprised her.

He could have picked solids or plaids, but no, he had chosen colorful parrots for one, tropical fish for another.

She picked up the third one, with fabric that had teddy bears picnicking, and held it tight to her. She would not take it apart and redo it. She would not sell it, even for a million dollars. She would keep it to remember him by, in case the price of capturing his lips with her own turned out to be that she never saw him again.

And she would not regret that kiss, even if that was the price of it.

CHAPTER FOURTEEN

THE NEXT DAY, Trixie felt as if she was holding her breath, waiting to see what would happen next.

Obviously, Daniel could see she had learned to cope with her injury and work around it. Obviously, he knew she did not need him anymore. What would it mean if he still came back?

But he didn't come back. He usually arrived first thing in the morning, and when she did not hear his familiar knock at the door, she felt like a balloon slowly deflating. Not even a phone call.

But then, what right did she have to have any expectations of him at all?

He arrived at noon, and Trixie began to breathe again. Did he seem sheepish, as if he had tried to stay away and could not?

No, she was reading too much into it. For her own survival, she had to stay in this world they had created: a world of moment by moment laughter and enjoyment. If she tried to move toward the future, it felt as if she would risk it all.

Daniel had another surprise for them. This time it was a Frisbee. That afternoon they chased after a bright neon pink Frisbee and each other, and the girls, until they were all in a tangled heap of limbs on the green, green, grass of the park, surrounded by sunlight, and the smell of lilacs, and laughing until they were choking on it.

The Frisbee got stuck in a tree, and Daniel unhesitatingly climbed up after it. The girls stood at the bottom, yelling instructions at him, while Trixie went back to the car to retrieve water bottles.

A lady, walking her dog, paused and smiled at Trixie.

"Your husband is so good with your children. I've been watching him the last few days. Some men are born to be daddies. You're a lucky woman."

Trixie was going to correct her. Daniel was not her husband. The girls were not her children. He would certainly deny he was born to be a daddy!

And yet, Trixie was so aware that she was a lucky woman, even if the future was uncertain! When was the future certain, anyway? So, she just smiled and let it go, savoring the feeling of luck and joy and being totally engaged in life.

She felt like a princess who had been asleep, who had been sleepwalking her way through life, going through the motions, but not quite there, not quite engaged.

Just like the sleeping princess, that kiss had made her come fully awake. She was fully alive and fully connected.

And that feeling was still deep inside her that night as they all squeezed onto one single bed, girls freshly bathed, hair wet—and still uncombed—fighting for places on his lap. Trixie squeezed up against his shoulder listening with pleasure to his deep voice reading the story.

Daniel never read the stories the way they were written! Always embellishing and adding funny accents, and asides and commentaries, until they were all nearly hysterical with laughter.

Some men were born to be daddies. The phrase kept running through her head, with the oddest insistence, but she put it aside to enjoy the way she felt right now. Her apartment strangely silent, she took the easy chair and Daniel collapsed on the sofa.

"Did we really get them to bed before ten o'clock?" he asked, glancing over at her with a smile.

Trixie returned his smile, marveling at, and savoring the ease between them. "We did." *We.* Like they were a team. A family, just as that passerby had thought they were. She should not be enjoying being a family so much! It wasn't true. It wasn't real. It was just temporary. He had made that plain last night!

And yet it felt like the most true, and most real thing she had ever done.

"Are we going to make some more cat-in-the-hats?" And then she blushed. How presumptuous to assume he was staying! And that he wanted to help her with her projects.

"Not tonight."

Trixie felt the stab of disappointment.

"I brought something to celebrate," he said.

And just like that, life felt good again.

"What are we celebrating?" she asked. *Besides the wonderful chance that life was going to surprise you in the most delicious of ways!* "I didn't see you bring anything in."

"Snuck it by you. It's in the fridge."

She got up and went to her fridge. Inside was a beautiful blue wine bottle. She took it out, snatched a corkscrew and two wineglasses—plastic, left over from the Champagne deliveries—and went back to the living room. This time she took the place right beside him on the sofa.

"It's ice wine," he said, reaching by her and taking it and the cork screw. "I've been saving it for a special occasion. And I was hoping for plastic glasses!"

She laughed. "The special occasion is tomorrow. The sling is coming off."

"No. The special occasion is right now."

Her heart felt as if it stood still. He was so right. The special moment was right now, him and her together, drinking in each other.

"Listen," he whispered.

She did. "I don't hear anything."

"That's what is special! Perfect silence. I think we need to drink a toast to that."

She actually thought that was a very bad idea. She'd seen what happened around him when her inhibitions were down!

He expertly uncorked the wine and poured some in her plastic glass. What could the harm be in one glass? To be adults together, enjoying the simple pleasure of sleeping children.

"Should we watch a movie?" she asked, feeling suddenly a little nervous about this time totally alone with him. Except for a few occasions, like that kiss last night, she could count on the twins to be a buffer between them, dissolving those moments of chemistry that leapt up unexpectedly when a hand touched, when eyes met.

"No," he said, and shot her a little smile that made a shiver dance along her spine.

Was it possible he *wanted* to spend time with her? That he wasn't just being a nice guy, who had found himself in a strange situation, and made the best of it?

He had come back, hadn't he? Even when last night had moved them into brand-new territory, shivering with unknown thrills. And dangers.

They settled in with their wine, the patio doors open to the summer air, scented from the lilacs that still bloomed in the front courtyard, warm and lovely on the skin. Wordlessly, they watched a spectacular summer sunset of the variety that Calgary was famous for.

Then they talked of small things: the girls, what they would have for dinner tomorrow; how they would go to a swimming pool after her doctor's appointment to have her sling removed.

She was aware of the deep comfort between them. She reached out, tentatively, and took his hand.

He didn't withdraw it.

"I don't know how to thank you for the last few days," she said.

"Don't be silly. No thanks are necessary."

And then, as she had known it would, the wine loosened her tongue. She thought of his ease with the girls and that lady commenting on how good he was with children. She thought of him reading, and knowing the perfect toys: bubble wands and water guns.

Suddenly, her sense of comfort dissolved.

She had to know where this was going. She could not be the woman she had been with Miles—always thinking about how to win his approval, always biting back saying the things she wanted to say, trying to gauge how he would take them.

Trixie realized she had to be willing to risk everything.

She was going to tell him she could see who he really was. And in doing so, she would be acknowledging who she really was.

She was really that girl who longed for a family. And a home. For the golden retriever. And the babies. Especially the babies.

He had made her strong enough to dream again. And to trust her dreams. And herself.

What she was about to say felt riskier than kissing him. Way riskier. But she had to say it. She was compelled to say it.

"Daniel," she said, "You know what a lady said to me today in the park? That you are a man who was born to be a daddy. And you know what? I agree with her. You were born to be a daddy."

* * *

You were born to be a daddy. Daniel felt panic shiver along his spine. He took a fortifying sip of his wine.

He knew he should not have come back here. Not after that kiss last night. The truth was he had tried to stay away.

And he couldn't. He'd seen that Frisbee in a store window, and thought of the joy it would bring the girls. When, exactly, had he stopped thinking of them as monsters, and started to delight in their delight?

He had thought of how Trixie was trying to cope, and he had thought of how much lighter he felt when he was with her.

He had thought of how life, without any of the accoutrements money could buy, had begun to shine as if lit from within.

Daniel had tried to stay away. He considered himself a man of amazing discipline. And yet, he could not fight what was unfolding here. He'd been compelled to come back.

But that statement jarred him. *You were born to be a daddy?* Good grief. That was his worst nightmare.

Or was it? Wasn't it what he had wanted once, more than anything else? When that long-ago girlfriend had told him she was pregnant, he had felt joy.

And hope.

Some small hope that he could have what others took for granted. A family.

He had shut down emotionally from the second that baby had gone from the world. And he had never wanted to open up again.

How was it that he, a man who thought out everything, and assessed possibility and looked constantly toward the future, had not seen this coming? That he was having fun, and Trixie was assessing his potential as a daddy?

Daniel was shocked that he had missed the most obvious of all conclusions: there were going to be consequences.

The bottle of wine had obviously been a mistake. No, it was all a mistake.

And it was time to set her straight. He had to come clean. He had known she wanted a fantasy. What had he been doing, playing along? Enjoying himself, kidding himself that he was helping her, when in the end, she was going to get hurt.

What amazed and shocked him, was that so was he.

It was time to let her know who he really was, before they got in this any deeper, before the damage was complete.

"No, really, I wasn't made to be a daddy," he said quietly.

"But you're so good with the kids."

Was there a bit of wistfulness in her voice?

He had always known he was going to have to end this, before she got hurt. Why had he played it out so long?

Why did it feel like her wistfulness was an echo of his own, for things he had decided he could not have?

It had been obvious things were getting more and more intense between them. His hand lingering on hers when she passed him the barbecue tongs.

Staying in those tangled heaps of limbs in the park longer than might have been strictly necessary.

Kissing over cookies. And then that soul-filling kiss last night.

Why hadn't he extricated himself long ago? It had nothing to do with Greta failing to find him a nanny.

He'd been enjoying this. Really? Or had he just found the perfect way to avoid his mother? Either way, it was all about him, and totally unfair to her. It was time to turn off that starry eyed look in Trixie's face.

It was time for a reality check.

There were a million ways he could have done it. He had letting women down gently down to an art.

But he'd never used the truth before. It startled him that he felt compelled to do so now.

"I don't have any desire to be a father," he said gruffly. "I don't have any desire to be a member of any kind of family unit."

"That's a lie," she said so firmly that for a moment he thought he saw a light shining in his darkness.

He fought the temptation to move toward it. Fought it with everything he had. For her protection. She deserved so much better.

"It's not in any way about you," he said, softly. "Trixie, it's all about me."

"Tell me why," she said, and she looked back at him, the tears gone, and a kind of bravery in her eyes that astounded him.

Was it possible this woman, tiny in size, was braver than he was?

Daniel sighed. He had always known, in some part of himself, that his secrets would not be safe from her. But maybe that was okay. When she knew the truth, that he was not a man to plan a future around, she could get on with her life. She, with her white picket fence dreams, would drop him faster than a hot coal.

"My Dad died when I was a baby," he said. "Nothing heroic. Just a run of the mill accident. He was skiing, he got lost in a snow storm. He never came home.

"My parents were young. They'd barely been married two years. They didn't have anything. He didn't even have life insurance.

"So, we were poor. My mom trying to scrape together a living. She wasn't educated. She wasn't really good at anything. She tried waitressing, and cleaning and working as a clerk in a store. But she was undisciplined. She couldn't get to work on time. She could not keep a job. So my early childhood memories are of a kind of desperation in every day. Where would we go when she couldn't pay the rent? What were we going to eat? One of my sharpest childhood memories from that time? My feet being freezing because we could not afford boots.

"Then, when I was about the same age as Molly and Pauline are now, she found a solution. His name was James. When she told me that man was going to be my dad, I was over the moon. I thought I finally got to be like all the other kids. That I'd get to play hockey and go fishing, and be released from my mother's world of soap operas on TV and *do I look pretty in this?*"

When had Trixie's hand found his? And why did it feel, not as if he were letting her go, but as if finally, finally, he had something to hold on to?

"At first, being part of a family was out of a

dream. The dream I dreamed. We had a nice house and did not move all the time. We had food. My mom stayed home. Maybe I even thought she was going to bake cookies. She never did. As a kid, I didn't know what was happening. As an adult, looking back, I can see while I was relishing the dream, she was getting restless."

He smiled wryly at Trixie, trying, still trying to hide something from her. A cold so deep, it felt as if it had frozen the place where his heart should be.

"See why I'm such a sucker for cookies?"

But Trixie seemed to be looking right by the smile. Her eyes were locked on his and she was *seeing* him. Her gaze, so direct, so giving, so compassionate was melting something that he was not sure he wanted melted.

"She never did bake cookies," he continued, hearing a rasp of unexpected emotion in his voice. "Or cook dinner. We ate takeout a lot. And I did get signed up for hockey, we did go fishing, James and I. Not my Mom. She had already kind of lost interest in the whole thing. In fact, she fell out of love with poor James with stunning swiftness. She was looking for something else or someone else. Something to *fill* her. It had never been me, and now it wasn't James, either.

"And so I became just part of the backdrop for arguments and smoldering silences and things getting thrown.

"James wasn't even completely out of the picture, before Kenneth was on scene. My *new* daddy. I think, for him, I still hoped, still wanted to believe."

"In love," Trixie whispered. "You wanted to believe in love."

"I guess," he said, wearily. "Love. Family. Home. But by daddy number four or five or six, I didn't have a single dream left. I was in survival mode. By the time I graduated from high school, I couldn't wait to get away from it all."

"But you still dreamed of a family," Trixie pointed out. "You still hoped didn't you? That's why you wanted to marry your girlfriend. That's why you wanted to have that baby?"

He snorted, but he felt a shiver that she could see that, when he had tried very hard not to.

"Well, that was the last kick at the can for me," he said grimly. "I've left fairy tales behind me, Trixie. That's why I'm not daddy material. Or husband material. Or family material."

"I don't believe you," she said stubbornly.

And he looked in her eyes, and he saw things there that made him not believe himself as entirely or as forcefully as he wanted to.

In the clearness of her eyes, he saw the life

he had always longed for. And that sensation of something melting around the region of his heart increased.

But he knew those kind of longings made a man weak, and not strong.

He knew that kind of hope left a person wide open to being hurt all over again.

"Look," he said, his voice gruff, "so-called love can turn to hate and disillusionment in the blink of an eye. It feels like I have lived through that cycle of hope to despair a million times. And it is the most destructive force in the whole universe. Ask your nieces, if you don't believe me."

But he quickly saw he had failed to frighten Trixie off.

He had failed to do anything, even convince himself. For rather than telling the story emphasizing his belief that love would go wrong and people would suffer, he felt strangely light for having trusted her with this part of himself.

She wasn't running. She looked as if she cared about him more, not less. She looked as if she was going to kiss him again!

He had told her the brutal truth, and the worst about himself, and she wasn't running.

But that only meant, he had to run for her. For both of them. He had to run from her. To protect them from all the endless and miserable possibilities that the force called love introduced to a life.

He closed his eyes, trying to block out what he felt when she looked at him. He withdrew his hand from hers.

Don't say one more word, Daniel ordered himself.

"She's getting married again," he said, his voice grim. "My mother is coming here with her latest beau, and she's getting married again. She wants me to be part of it."

"And will you?" Trixie asked softly.

It made him feel angry. Hadn't she heard anything he said? Of course she had. But she was one of those types: the type who would go on dreaming and hoping and extending the hand of compassion and forgiveness no matter what.

She was one of those types who would require you to be a better man every single day of your life.

He'd known the truth all along. He was not worthy of her. Not even close. He was damaged.

There was a possibility that long-ago girlfriend, who had married the doctor, had seen what was true about him all along.

"You—and the girls—have been a great diversion," he said, with deliberate harshness. "You've helped me not think about my mother at all, helped me avoid her barrage of phone calls and texts.

"But your sling is coming off tomorrow. You don't need me anymore. I'm leaving now, and I'm not coming back."

Her mouth opened in disbelief. He thought she was going to cry, and that he was going to hate himself.

But her mouth snapped shut and a fire sparked in her eyes.

"You know what?" she said. "Good. Go. And don't come back! You don't have a clue who you really are."

Her response stunned him. And intrigued him.

"What do you mean I don't have a clue who I am? I do so."

"No, you don't. You're not a man too cowardly to go talk to your mother, for God's sake."

Cowardly? It was his turn for his mouth to fall open.

"And something else? You *were* born to be a daddy. You were in absolute bliss every second you spent with those kids. Or maybe your experiences made you the perfect father. Because of what you have been through, you know at your deepest level what kids need. And you love giving it to them. But if you want to miss that? If you want to fill every second of your pathetic life with the headlong pursuit of the superficial, you go for it. That's your problem. I feel sorry for you."

His mouth was still hanging open. He wanted to slap his ears with the palm of his hand to make sure he had heard correctly.

Trixie Marsh had just called his life pathetic! Trixie Marsh felt sorry for him!

"Don't let the door hit you on the way out," she said, and got up off the couch, pushed by him, went down the hall and closed her bedroom door with quiet finality behind her.

He went through the kitchen, and tried not to look at the picture on her fridge of a bedroom painted with black walls and with a zebra skin rug. He'd underestimated her in every way. Maybe she was going to have that room after all.

In the hall he fought the temptation to go down it and take one last peek at those innocent sleeping girls.

He was irritated with how right Trixie was. Damn it, he had loved every moment of being with them!

He went out the apartment door, locked the handle and then closed it quickly behind him. So that the cat wouldn't get out.

And so that he wouldn't hear how loudly she was not crying.

CHAPTER FIFTEEN

TRIXIE SAT ON the edge of her bed, staring at her hands. They were trembling in reaction to the fight. She heard her apartment door close behind Daniel.

She couldn't believe what she had just done!

And what she really could not believe was that she was glad she had done it!

How far she had come from the girl who had been dumped by her only boyfriend. Calling him *begging* him to rethink it, to give her another chance.

"Ohmygod," she muttered, "I almost gave Miles another chance." Something shivered along her spine. Pure gratitude that Miles had had the good sense not to come back!

Would she give Daniel another chance?

Of course. She realized they had just had their first major fight. Would they recover from it? She knew, if they didn't, or couldn't, or wouldn't, that there had not been enough there to begin with.

And something in her heart whispered to her that there was enough there. More than enough.

That love was there.

And that love was always enough.

And that even though it was the thing Daniel was most afraid of, she knew who he was, even if he didn't.

And he was brave enough to say yes to love.

She just knew it.

But her confidence in that conclusion was shaken when he didn't call the next day. Or the day after that.

Well, he was stubborn. It was going to take him a while to figure it all out. And she was going to wait. And have some pride. What she wasn't going to do was phone him, *begging*.

She shuddered at the woman she used to be.

And looked, in utter amazement, at the woman she had become over the past few days. Alive. Fun-loving. Caring. Trixie Marsh had become the woman she always wanted to be. A woman thoroughly deserving of love.

And worthy of every one of her dreams.

Still, when Daniel did not return, the twins were worse than ever! Mourning yet another loss. Trixie had her hands full trying to keep them occupied. She tried it all: bubble wands and Frisbees, but the twins were having none of it.

"Want Dan-man!"

Three days after she had thrown him out of the apartment, she had finally gotten the twins into bed. They were sleeping fitfully. She was dozing on the couch.

There was a soft knock on her door.

Trixie woke and glanced at the time. It was eleven o'clock at night! Trixie raced to it, her heart in her throat.

He knew. He had come back.

Trixie opened the door to find her sister standing outside it. Abby looked sunburned and she had mosquito bites all over her face. Her hair was a mess. Her arms were covered with scratches. She had obviously been crying. Lots. There was a duffel bag at her feet, and she just left it there, in the hallway, and staggered past her sister, through the apartment and fell across the couch.

She lay there, arm thrown dramatically over her forehead, eyes squeezed shut.

"The girls are sleeping," Trixie said, coming into the living room after dragging the duffel bag out of the hallway.

"Oh. Good. I can't deal with them right now."

Trixie frowned at that. Those children were gifts!

"How was your trail ride?" Trixie ventured.

"Exhausting. Hard. Horrible. Uncomfortable."

"Oh."

"It was bloody horrible, just like my life!"

And then her sister was sobbing, and Trixie went over, and made her sit up and put her arms around her.

And the whole story came out. Her husband, Warren, had been busy all the time. He never helped her. He never seemed to realize how hard it was being at home all day with the kids. She needed his support. She needed to know he loved her.

And when that hadn't happened, she had started playing around on the internet. As Trixie had suspected, she had found adventure online. Though, not in quite the way Trixie had thought!

Abby had found a job with a company that led trail rides through the Canadian wilderness. It had helped that the lead wrangler was sexy as all get out!

"Sam offered to give me a trial. I've always wanted to work with horses," she said defiantly at Trixie's appalled look.

"You've never had a single thing to do with horses!" Trixie protested.

"I thought I was going to come home to Canada and start a new life. That Sam would fall madly in love with me, and it would be the most wildly romantic thing that ever happened to me."

Trixie bit her tongue not to remind Abby she was a mother with children!

But Abby had learned her own lessons. She had quickly discovered what had existed online was not in any way real, and that, while maybe going on a trail ride through the Rockies would be romantic, working on one was not. And it certainly was not any way to start a new relationship.

"Sam was awful. Cuter than I expected, but critical. A slave driver. A perfectionist," Abigail sobbed. "He wanted a girl who could shoe horses, and throw a saddle and then put a meal together over a campfire. For sixteen hungry people. He fired me!"

Trixie decided now was not the time to compare wounds over being fired. It was time to practice her new skill of telling it how it was.

"What are you going to do, Abigail?" Trixie asked softly. "Your first responsibility is to your children. And Warren struck me as being such a good guy. You need to give him another chance. The girls are lost without their daddy."

"Me give him another chance? Oh my god, Trixie, he'll never give me another chance. He'll never forgive me for this. I've done a terrible thing. Not just with the cowboy. I mean nothing happened between us, but when I left I thought it might! And I took the girls and just left. I—I deceived him. I knew he'd look here first, so in the note I left, I led him to believe I'd taken the kids to my girlfriend, Mindy's. She lives in South Africa."

"You need to go home," Trixie said. She wondered when she had become such an expert on what other people needed. "How could you do something so dreadful to that poor man?"

Not that other people seemed to appreciate it. At all.

Because her sister looked at her, and said, stubbornly, "I already feel guilty enough without you acting as my conscience! And I'm not going home. To what? I'm staying right here."

"Here?" Trixie squeaked.

"In Canada. But yes, here, with you. Just until I get on my feet."

"You need to at least call Warren and tell him where you are."

Her sister looked stricken. "I've been trying him on every phone I could get my hands on. I can't find him."

"What?"

"I suspect," she said sadly, "he's combing every corner of South Africa."

* * *

Daniel didn't like the boutique hotel as much as he remembered liking it. The reason he had moved out of Kevin's apartment was ironic.

The pitter-patter of little feet.

Only now, that sound had caused a deep longing in him. It sounded like things were out of control up there.

He had to fight down the compulsion to go check. To go help.

It would only confirm, in Trixie's mind, her totally erroneous conclusion that was born to be a daddy.

About that she had been so wrong. About other things she couldn't have been more right. Because in response to what the pitter-patter of little feet did to his heart, Daniel did the utterly cowardly thing. He moved.

But the hotel wasn't what he remembered. First class, yes. But also impersonal. Almost sterile. The hushed quiet had a deathly feel to it, and he found himself pining for liveliness.

And he didn't like work as much as he remembered liking it, either. How could the things he had lived for suddenly seem dull? Unimportant?

He felt as if he was going through the motions. As if his world had gone from full living color to sepia.

His phone rang. The other phone. Mother.

He took a deep breath, and looked around the empty opulence of his hotel suite.

How's avoidance working for you so far? he asked himself wryly.

Daniel answered the phone. His mother was so shocked to have a real person on the line that she was absolutely silent.

Which he took advantage of.

"Mom, I'm going to fly into Montreal. Tomorrow. We need to talk."

"But I'll be there in Calgary for the wedding in just a few days! Daniel. You've been impossible! We have so much to do. I want your shirt to match—"

"That's what I need to talk to you about."

"You don't want to come to my wedding," she said, her tone hurt. "That's why you've been avoiding me."

Ya think?

"I'll see you tomorrow."

"Daniel—"

He hung up on her. But gently.

CHAPTER SIXTEEN

DANIEL SAT ACROSS the table from his mother in one of Montreal's finest restaurants. She was astoundingly beautiful, as always, but he saw she had aged substantially since he had seen her a year ago. She looked fragile, somehow, more frail than he remembered her being.

"Have you met someone?" she asked him eagerly.

He repressed the desire to groan out loud. Thankfully, it was a standard question. She was not that astute.

"No, Mom." It felt like a lie on his tongue, bitter tasting. Because he had met someone. No, not really *met*. Been thrust into someone's life.

"Oh," she looked disappointed. "Everything else is okay?"

"Sure. Why do you ask?"

She shrugged, but her eyes remained on his face. "I don't know. You look tired. Strained."

More astute than he'd given her credit for,

then. Because he was tired. Despite being surrounded by the sumptuous silence of the op-
ulent suite at the boutique hotel, he was not
sleeping well.

"I need to talk to you about your wedding,
Mom."

She hunched her shoulders, as if waiting for
a blow.

"I don't want to stand up with you," he said
softly. "I don't want to be your man of honor."

"But why?" she asked plaintively.

It amazed him that she had to ask!

"You'll love Phillip," she said quickly. "He—"

"Mom, don't you get it? I've heard all of this
a thousand times before."

She looked stricken.

"I don't believe it, okay? I can't stand up beside you as an affirmation of your belief in love.
To me, it's all a giant fairy tale. The one that
never comes true."

"You don't believe in love?" she whispered.

He snorted gently. "Come on, Mom. The
question shouldn't be whether I believe in love,
it should be how can you? How many times up
to the altar now. Seven? Or is this eight? And
that doesn't count all the boyfriends."

*Who had the good sense to run before they
became ensnared in a web of dreams that was
clearly impossible to fulfill.*

"It doesn't exist," he said softly. "Mom, this thing you are chasing endlessly after does not exist. And I can't stand beside you, one more time, pretending it does, watching you vow it does. Standing up with you means I *agree*."

"It does exist," she said. She had ducked her head and was going through her purse, and he couldn't be sure he had heard her.

"What?"

"It does exist," she said. She found a tissue, dabbed at her eyes, put it away and snapped her purse shut. She lifted her chin and looked him right in the eye. "It does exist, and don't you dare say it doesn't."

"Mom! You dragged me through it with you!"

"Because I wanted you to know it!" she said sharply. "I didn't want you to live without it. I knew what it was. I had it. I didn't want to exist if I couldn't have it again. I wanted it for you."

"What are you talking about?"

"I'm talking about love," she said, softly, reverently. "And I'm talking about your dad. There has never been anything like that for me again. I loved that man madly. And he loved me the same way. It felt as if the very air sang with joy when we were together. It felt as if I was alive, more than alive, as if every moment quivered with the most exquisite light. I could *feel*. Everything. If a bird flew by me, I could feel the puffs of air coming off its wings."

Daniel felt a shiver along his spine, and it seemed to him the room filled up with the scent of lilacs. His mother was describing the way he had felt over the days with Trixie.

"When he died," she said, softly, "when my beloved David died, I thought I would die, too. The grief was so intense I did not know how I could survive it. I couldn't even hold a job or think straight about how to get bills paid and food on the table for you. I was such a mess."

Guiltily, Daniel remembered telling Trixie his mom had been undisciplined.

"I contemplated not going on," she admitted. "More than once. I just wanted to be with him.

"But you kept me here. You, and this feeling that I had. A feeling that I needed to give you what I'd had. I was driven by a sense that if I failed at that, I had failed completely. As a mother." She stopped, and then finished softly, "At life."

She met his gaze proudly. "You see it as a string of pathetic failures. But I saw it as a quest. A mission."

"Aw, Mom."

"I haven't succeeded," she said sadly. "If I

had, you would be with a woman who made you laugh and set your heart on fire, and I would be bouncing grandbabies on my knee. Instead of making you see how necessary love was to the art of breathing, I did the exact opposite. I made you afraid."

Coward, Trixie had hurled at him.

And it occurred to him, now, for the first time, that Trixie had been absolutely right.

And that his mother, flawed as she was, had one of the bravest, strongest and most hopeful hearts he had ever seen.

He picked up her hand, tenderly, lifted it to his lips, and kissed it.

"I'll stand up for you," he said, his voice husky.

It was the exact opposite of what he had come here to do. And yet, it did not feel like a defeat. It felt as if he was getting something that he had always missed before.

Sometimes, when you loved, putting the other person first came as naturally as breathing.

"Maybe I looked in all the wrong places," she conceded softly, something broken in her voice. "I should have realized that loving you, his son, could be enough for me. I guess I didn't believe it could be enough for you. Why is it we have to get old before we understand anything at all?"

Was he going to wait until he got old to understand all the important things?

"Let's finish lunch," he said, still holding her hand. "And then we'll go shopping for that shirt you want me to wear. One to match Phillip's."

His mother beamed at him, as if he had made the sun come out in her world.

He realized he wasn't a hurt little boy, anymore, coming to her filled with neediness. He was a man, whole and complete. Nothing she could do or say could fill him up. Or empty him out.

For the first time in his life, Daniel felt ready for love. Genuine love.

And he knew why he felt that way. And he knew who he felt that way about.

But the question was, did he have the smallest amount of his mother's bravery in him? Enough to go after it? Or would he stay in his comfort zone?

Would he stay in a world that seemed to have been drained of its color and excitement, that seemed suddenly and sadly sterile and stale? But that was, ultimately safe?

He was a man who made important decisions readily, with confidence. Without hesitation. It said something to him, about love, that he seemed unable to make a decision.

And he decided to wait until after his mother's wedding, as if something essential, that he needed to know about love, would reveal itself to him then.

CHAPTER SEVENTEEN

THERE WERE ALWAYS last minute panics at his mother's vow exchanges. This time it was flowers.

"I ordered lilacs," she sobbed. "I wanted simplicity. What could be more simple than that?"

Daniel bit his tongue. Who ordered lilacs? They grew in trees.

"Never mind," he said. "I'll look after it."

"You don't even know what a lilac looks like."

That might have been true a few weeks ago. Now, he knew exactly what they looked like and exactly where to find them. Harrington Place, the apartment building he had been avoiding since his return from his meeting with his mother in Montreal.

"I got it," he said, relieved to be going out the door. His mother's tension was all too familiar.

But it was replaced with a different kind of tension as he approached the apartment building.

Would he see Trixie? What would he say

to her? Molly and Pauline must be gone back home by now.

He felt sad when he thought of that. He might never see them again. Why hadn't he made a point of going over and saying goodbye?

Because seeing them would have forced his hand. Trixie, ultraintuitive, would have *known* something was up with him. Seeing Trixie would force his hand, too. He would have answer his questions about love way before he was ready to answer them!

He got out of his car in the no parking zone in front of the apartment. The lilacs, he noticed, were almost done. But there were a few good stems left, if he dug deep inside the shrub.

Feeling conspicuous in his tux, he took a pocketknife out of his glove compartment and buried himself in the trees, trying to get a few flowers that weren't sagging completely.

As he was in amongst the lilacs, a cab roared up.

At first he didn't pay it any mind. But then a man's voice—the heavy Australian accent, the note of fury in it—caught his attention.

Daniel peered out of the shrub.

The man was gigantic. If Daniel had a single doubt about who it was, the hair clinched it. The man had a head of hair as black and curly as Pauline's and Molly's. And it looked every bit as uncombed, a wild tangle that seemed to match the desperation in his face.

Daniel watched as he went up to the apartment door, tried it, and found it locked. He began to pound on it, as if unaware of the intercom system beside it.

The hair stood up on Daniel's neck. He hadn't felt this way since he had heard a loud thump in the night. He stepped from the bushes, lilacs in hand.

"Can I help you?"

The man took in the lilacs and tuxedo. He looked at the door as if he planned to kick it in.

Without betraying it with so much as a flicker, not even setting down the flowers, Daniel could feel himself moving into a warrior-mode: ready. Ready to protect Trixie with his own life, if need be.

"I'm looking for my kids," the man said. "I'm hoping they're here with their aunt."

Daniel's inner red alert slid down the danger scale a notch. The man looked tormented, afraid for his children.

"Molly and Pauline?" he asked.

"How do you know that?"

"It's a long story."

"Are they here?"

There was something so wretched in the

man's face, that Daniel's red alert downgraded yet again.

"They were. Visiting their aunt Trixie. I don't know if they are, anymore. I have a key to that door. Let's go find out." Daniel felt relieved that he now had a modicum of control over the encounter.

They rode the elevator up together. Daniel knocked on that familiar door. On the other side of it they could hear the shrieking of children gone completely wild. Small feet stampeded by on the other side of the door. Daniel cast a glance at the man beside him.

A funny little smile had started to play on his features. Daniel had to knock louder to be heard above the noise.

Trixie came and opened the door. She looked gorgeous. She looked like the most beautiful being he had ever seen. He realized her hair had grown since they had first met. She had the dandelion fluff stems tamed with bobby pins. It made her look about twelve—and adorable.

Besides looking beautiful, Trixie looked harried. And utterly exhausted. She took in Daniel and the flowers, and a tiny smile lit her features. Her gaze moved to the man beside him.

"Warren! I wasn't expecting you." Her greeting was surprised, but friendly. In fact, the big, bristling man barely held her attention, so she obviously felt no threat from him.

Daniel let go of any remaining thought that he might have to come to her rescue. Was he disappointed? He realized, abashed, he *liked* rescuing her, playing knight to her damsel in distress!

Crazily, Daniel held out the flowers he had picked for his mother to Trixie, as if that had been his intention all along. Trixie hesitated for just a split second, then stepped into the hall and took the lilacs, buried her nose in their scent. She looked shy and pleased. She slid him a look.

Could it be possible? Was that look loaded with the thing he had always feared the most? Did she love him?

Why did it feel wonderful, instead of terrifying?

Warren, impatient, pushed forward and stepped in the door. "Molly? Pauline?"

The rampaging of small feet halted. The silence was instant. And then the girls came running.

"Daddy!" they shrieked in unison.

And that big man went down on his knees and gathered his children in his arms. He was a powerful man who had been brought to his knees by this thing called love.

But then he was lifted up by that same force. He rose up, lifting his children, one in each arm, as if they weighed nothing at all. He was made powerful again—maybe, if the light that shone in his face was any indication, more powerful than he had ever been before, made stronger by whatever he had endured at love's hand.

Warren turned in a joyous circle, the girls clinging to the column of his neck, and swung them around until the purest of joy shone in the air around them. Daniel had to blink to make sure he was seeing correctly.

There was no light on in the hallway. It was probably the darkest space in the whole apartment.

And yet the space seemed drenched in light.

Daniel glanced at Trixie and saw she was mesmerized by the purity of what they were seeing.

Finally, the giant of a man set his girls down, settled his huge hands on top of their heads with exquisite tenderness, drank in those upturned faces with gratitude and wonder. "What's with the hair, my two little monkeys?"

"Nobody combs our hair but you!" Molly said fiercely.

"Ah," he said, with astounding softness for a man who looked so rough around the edges. "You'd better fetch me your brush, then."

It was only when the girls had scampered away that Daniel noticed the other woman. She looked just like Trixie, and yet Daniel knew he would never have to put a dot on Trixie's nose to tell them apart.

It was obvious from the way she was dressed, that Abby was flashier. There was something in the tilt of her head that hinted at restlessness, and uncertainty.

They were identical, so how was it he felt Trixie was the lovelier of the two? Softer, radiating a truth about who she was, whether she knew it or not.

Her sister, Abby, stood in the shadows of the hallway, away from the light, her arms folded defensively across her chest, rigid with tension.

Warren saw her, and everything in him froze.

It went very still. It seemed to Daniel, as if that light he had seen, was flickering now, threatening to go out.

The man and woman stood staring at each other for the longest time.

And then the man lifted his arms, palms up, *come to me*.

And Abby flew into that small invitation, that hint of forgiveness, and burrowed herself under Warren's arm, and sobbed into his chest.

The strong, strong man, ran his hands through her hair, cradled her against him, turned ever so slightly to take her more fully to himself.

And when he turned, Daniel saw his face.

And in it, he had the answer he had searched for his whole life.

The look on the man's face—peaceful, accepting, forgiving—confirmed what he had suspected after witnessing his mother's eternal hopefulness.

That it was worth it.

That love was worth it. Love was worth walking through the fire. It was worth the pain of the burns.

It was worth it for this moment, when love was rising phoenixlike from the ashes, made stronger, a testament to the unending hope and utter wonder that composed the miracle that was life.

Daniel reached out and closed the apartment door, softly, with him and Trixie on the other side of it.

He realized he wanted her to go to the wedding with him.

Oh, God. If he showed up at his mother's wedding with a woman—especially a woman like Trixie—his mother would practically take it as posting of the banns.

But for the first time since he had moved into the boutique hotel, Daniel's world felt right.

For the first time since he'd had lunch with his mother in Montreal, the doubts fled him. And the questions. His mind didn't have a single thing to say.

But his heart did. His heart had a whole lot to say. And Daniel listened, and then he knew exactly what to do.

And so he did it.

"Want to go to a wedding?"

Trixie, still clutching her lilacs, laughed shakily, and looked down at her bare feet. "I'm not dressed for a wedding. And I am not going back in there."

Indeed, she was not dressed for a wedding, especially since his mother had chosen the most expensive venue in Calgary. Trixie was in shorts and a T-shirt and bare feet. Her toenails were freshly painted in that delectable pink.

It was almost exactly what she'd been wearing the first time he had seen her.

"Details," he said. "We have time to go get you something to wear."

She hesitated.

"The option," he said softly, nodding toward the closed door, "is to go back in there." Of course, there was another option. She could say no.

He was aware he was holding his breath,

waiting for her answer. He was aware it was not about going to a wedding together, at all.

It was about saying yes to a journey into the unknown. Travelling pathways that led who knew where. Sometimes frightening, sometimes trying, and always, always leading to the fullest glory a human being could ever know.

CHAPTER EIGHTEEN

TRIXIE STOOD IN the hallway in her bare feet, hugging her flowers, and riding the wave of what she had just witnessed between Abigail and Warren.

When she looked into Daniel's face, she saw a reflection of that very same light.

She ordered herself to stop and think about this. She couldn't just cast herself on him because he had showed up with wilted lilac blossoms and a tux! Where was her pride?

Wouldn't that be the same thing she had done with Miles? Begged for love? Accepted any crumb of affection as a substitute for the real thing?

But she cast a look at the door, and she knew she wasn't going back in there. Whatever was happening in there was personal, of the extreme variety.

"I don't even have my purse," she said, not

wanting to give in too easily. "I don't even have shoes."

He glanced at his watch. "We can go shopping."

"I just told you, I don't have my purse."

He cocked his head at her, studied her, and then smiled. "I don't suppose you could consider it a gift?"

"No. Absolutely not, no."

His smile deepened.

She didn't feel like she was begging for love. She didn't feel that one little bit. She felt as if she was being seen. She smiled back at him, feeling tentativeness slide into boldness.

He gathered Trixie in his arms, crushing the lilacs between them. And he kissed her hello.

It seemed like long, breathless moments later, he was leading her out to his car. He stopped to pluck more lilacs from the center of the shrubs, then tossed them behind his seat.

It was the first time she had ridden in Daniel's car, up until this point the presence of the twins had necessitated the use of hers.

The car was sleek and powerful and expensive.

"Could we have the top down?" she ventured.

"It'll wreck your hair."

She didn't care. The top slid down, and as the wind grabbed her slightly longer locks, she pulled out the bobby pins and cast them to the wind. They sped over to an upscale mall. He scanned the storefronts and guided her toward one called Flame.

"I can't shop here," she said, digging in her bare heels and still clutching her lilacs.

"Look, we have ten minutes to get to the church on time, so it's shop here, or hold up a wedding. I think that's bad luck or something." He pulled out his phone, pretended to put something in, squinted at the screen. "Definitely bad luck."

She gulped and ducked in the door with him.

She felt the salesclerk give her bare feet and shorts a very snooty look—and then take one look at Daniel and change into something completely different, helpful, considerate, polite.

"We're in a hurry. Dress for a small afternoon wedding. Private room at the Palace Garden."

His naming of the premier hotel in Calgary said everything the clerk needed to know.

The woman, catching the urgency, pointed Trixie toward a changeroom. What happened next was straight out of a fairy tale, Cinderella being outfitted for the ball. In seconds, Trixie found herself in her skivvies, with three dresses thrust into her hands. She looked hurriedly for price tags and found none.

She slipped into the first, turned and looked at herself in the mirror. It was blue, off the shoulder, calf-length, gauzy and gorgeous.

She went out and showed it to Daniel, who was waiting in a chair. He looked at her appraisingly, shook his head. She was going to protest—the dress was gorgeous, perfect for the occasion—but it was true she didn't feel any zing from it. Besides, there was no time for argument.

The second dress was pale peach chiffon with a matching jacket. Again, she modeled, again it was rejected with a faint shake of his head. She was glad about the rejection of that one: it made her feel like a matron aunt!

She slid on the third dress. It was an amazing harmony of violets: the palest lavender swirling into the deepest indigo. It was narrow-strapped and V-necked, and it ended mid-thigh, making her look long-legged and, dared she say, sexy? Her heart was pounding when she went out the door to see Daniel's reaction to it.

He stared at her. A look came on in his eyes that she could not have dreamed in her wildest dreams. A look that was for her!

His mouth fell open.

He smacked it shut, covered it with his hand, and said, reverently, "Well, I'll be gobsmacked."

And then, to the consternation of the clerk,

they were both killing themselves laughing. The outfit was quickly completed with shoes and a clutch. Daniel insisted on going into the jewelry store next door and buying a necklace and matching earrings.

He showed them to her.

"Those better not be real diamonds," she said. She hoped to sound firm. She was fairly certain she sounded wistful instead.

With sure fingers, he placed the necklace around her neck, and then, with exquisite gentleness inserted each earring in her pierced lobes.

He smiled with satisfaction. "From the first second I saw those ears, those are the earrings I pictured in them."

She'd been about to argue she couldn't possibly afford them. Now she closed her mouth with a snap. If she had to eat macaroni and cheese for a year, it would be worth it for the look on his face as he admired her ears.

At her insistence, they stopped at a drugstore, and aware of all eyes on her—and aware that such attention made her feel something she had never felt, gorgeous—she picked up new pins for her hair.

And while Daniel sped to the hotel, fighting the wind, she scraped the little bit of hair she had back from her face, and pinned it up.

Daniel's mother was beautiful. When she met Trixie, her look was appraising, and then something relaxed in it. She looked oddly satisfied.

She oohed and aahed over the drooping lilacs Daniel had retrieved from his backseat as if it was a bouquet of rare African orchids.

The wedding was lovely, simple and classic, a beautiful ceremony, followed by a private dinner for a few friends.

"It won't last," he said, much later as they were leaving.

"But I hope it does," Trixie said.

He was silent, and then he said, "You know what? Me, too. You know what she told me? That she is on a quest. That she had perfect love with my dad, and she's not dying without finding that again."

"It's kind of beautiful, isn't it? That kind of hope?" Trixie whispered.

"Yeah," he whispered back, "It kind of is."

And that was how Daniel Riverton began his slow wooing of Trixie Marsh. Warren and Abby and the twins went home to Australia and his mother and Phillip returned to Montreal. Daniel moved back into Kevin's apartment. He liked being close to Trixie.

It meant barbecues at her place, and working on her orders for cat-in-the-hats. It meant blowing bubbles off her balcony.

It meant watching *When Harry Met Sally* until they knew the entire script by heart. They reenacted the restaurant scene—but only in the privacy of one of their apartments—until they were rolling on the floor with laughter.

Over the hot days of summer Daniel's and Trixie's life melted together as effortlessly and beautifully as the chocolate fudge ripple ice cream they both loved so much.

They went to the Calgary Stampede and cheered on their favorite chuck wagons, they rode the highest Ferris wheel at the midway, they ate cotton candy and corn dogs and he threw baseballs at milk jugs until he won her a stuffed pink gorilla as big as she was.

When the Stampede ended, they found cool creeks to swim in, and private wooded areas in which to have picnics. They strolled the beautiful shaded pathways along the Bow River as evenings fell.

He accepted her little envelopes with payments in them: for the food from Champagne, for the dress and shoes from Flame.

But he drew the line at the diamond necklace and earrings.

What he never did was bring her to his loft. Instead, he took the picture off her fridge and slipped it into his pocket. Trixie never even noticed it was gone.

Angelica was not happy to be starting all over again, but he didn't care if Angelica was happy. He paid the bills. Plus, starting all over meant he got to stay at Kevin's even longer.

They rode bicycles and played with kittens and puppies in pet stores. He bought himself a goldfish, named him Harvey, and fed him religiously. Daniel bought a plant, too, testing himself to see if he could be trusted with living things.

And as summer eased into fall both the goldfish and the plant were still alive.

"Angelica tells me they're giving me back the loft at the end of next week," Daniel announced one fall evening. "She wants to do a big reveal. A cocktail party."

If it had been Miles, Trixie knew she would be jealous. Or suspicious. Or both.

When had she come to feel so secure? So loved?

"Will you come?"

"Of course!"

At the end of the next week, Trixie took a private elevator up to the loft, struggling with a large potted plant. She stepped off the elevator directly into Daniel's space.

It was absolutely stunning. It was a huge open area, anchored by original brick walls, and original floor to ceiling eyebrow windows.

There was a state of the art kitchen in the open area, and Daniel was there, opening a bottle of wine. It occurred to her the backsplash and granite countertops in the kitchen were solid black. The cabinets and trim were sleek white.

She studied it. It was beautiful and sleek, and there was something vaguely familiar about it.

It wasn't until she turned her attention to the living room that she got it.

Two black couches faced each other over a zebra rug.

"Daniel, it's like the picture," Trixie stammered, setting the plant down. He came and handed her a wine.

"Yes," he said. "It's just like your picture."

It occurred to her they were alone. "I thought it was some sort of big reveal, like a cocktail party."

"There was only one person I wanted to reveal it to," he said huskily. "And that was you."

"It's beautiful," she said, "like something out of a dream." But she wasn't looking at his refurbished apartment at all. She was looking straight at him.

"It doesn't feel beautiful to me," he said softly. "It feels empty. Harvey isn't proving as good company as I thought he'd be."

He was watching her, his eyes faintly hooded,

smoldering with something that made her heart beat way too fast.

"How can you say that?" Her eyes moved from exquisite furniture to amazing fixtures. "That piece of art over the sofa, on the brick? Amazing!"

"That doesn't matter to me."

Suddenly, she felt his intensity, saw that he was looking at nothing but her.

"Daniel, what is it?" she whispered. She reached up and touched his familiar and beloved face with her fingertips.

"It's you," he said, turning his head ever so slightly so that his lips grazed her fingertips.

"Me?" she squeaked. She wished he would quit doing that thing to her fingers. She couldn't think straight.

Actually, she hoped he would never stop doing that thing to her fingers. Thinking straight was overrated. Way.

"All this stuff doesn't matter to me. Only one thing in this room feels truly beautiful to me."

She felt as if she couldn't breathe. He stopped nuzzling her fingers, and then Daniel sank down on one knee, reached into his pocket, pulled out a velvet box and opened it.

"I don't even want to live here if you aren't going to live here with me."

She could not speak. She touched the box,

watched, entranced, as he took the ring, and tenderly took her finger.

"Will you marry me, Trixie?"

She nodded mutely. He slid the ring onto her finger. The sparkle of the diamond was nearly blinding, but not nearly as blinding as the light in his eyes.

Then he stood up, gathered her in his arms, and lifted her. He swung her around until the walls echoed with his laughter and her shrieks of delight.

"No neighbors," he said, placing his forehead on hers, and doing that wonderful wicked thing with his eyebrows.

"That's good," she said. "Because twins run in my family."

"You should have told me that before I proposed," he growled.

"Why, are you chicken?"

"No," he said, suddenly solemn. "I'm not. I've never felt braver or stronger or more certain in my entire life."

"I love you," she whispered.

He gathered her to him again, rested his chin on the top of her head, and said softly, "I'm absolutely gobsmacked by you, Trixie."

EPILOGUE

"Do you hear that?"

Daniel woke up, felt Trixie's soft, warm weight next to him, and smiled through the grogginess.

Did a man ever get used to this? Did he ever stop marveling at the wonder that had visited his world?

Trixie nudged him again. He turned and looked at her, gathered her to him, pressed his face into the sweetness of her hair. His wife. Did a man ever tire of the sacredness of those words, and all they implied?

"Listen," she insisted.

He did as she asked. Ah. *The pitter-patter of little feet.*

He remembered, a long time ago, when he had been a different man in a different world, that he had not thought anyone who was actually subjected to the pitter-patter of little feet could ever use that expression with genuine affection.

Especially—he turned and looked at the clock beside his bed—at three in the morning, when the owners of said little feet should be in bed, fast asleep.

"Are they ever going to get turned around?" Trixie whispered. "I think this may have been a mistake."

He smiled, and turned his head to her again, gently pressed his thumb against the worry line in her brow.

"It wasn't a mistake. You've always wanted to see Australia. Your sister and Warren renewing their vows was the perfect reason to come. Plus, they are so eager to have the twins stay with them."

"I don't know about leaving the girls," Trixie worried in a whisper. "They are so turned around! It'll be a nightmare."

He chuckled at her anxiety. His mother and Phil had relocated to Calgary after the birth of the twins. They loved to babysit, and Trixie could sometimes even be convinced to leave the girls with them for a weekend. His mother and Phil were still astoundingly happy after four years of marriage.

But this would be Daniel and Trixie's first time spending more than a week—eight whole days—away from their three-year-old twin girls.

"Well, what goes around comes around," Daniel said softly. "It's payback time for Abby. She left her monsters with us, and now we're going to leave ours with her."

Trixie didn't look convinced.

"Besides," he said, reassuringly, "Molly and Pauline can't wait to spend time with their cousins. They fancy themselves helpers now that they are all of eight years old. Last time I spoke to them on the phone, they were so excited. They were picking out outfits for our twins, as if they were going to be presented with a pair of life-size dolls to play with."

"We could stay," Trixie said. "We could—"

"We could. But I'm looking forward to having a second honeymoon."

Her eyes locked on his, full of memories of the first one. That familiar heat blazed between them.

And was put out by the pitter-patter of little feet. He sighed, and rolled away from Trixie.

"Girls," he called, resigned. "Come here."

The bedroom door slid open. Two identical sets of wide eyes, the color of drooping purple pansies, regarded him. Hair like dark dandelion fluff scattered around pixie faces.

He smiled and that was the only invitation needed.

Carly and Kristen exploded through the

door, white nighties tangling around sturdy legs. They leapt onto the bed, climbed over him and inserted themselves right between him and Trixie.

"Can't sleep, huh?" he said.

"Nope." That was Carly. He had no doubt she, the one who had erupted into the world first, and been in the lead ever since, was the one who couldn't sleep and had woken her sister. What fun was being awake, if you had no one to share it with, after all?

Kristen snuggled into him, popped her thumb in her mouth, murmured around it, "Daddy, do you think Harvey misses me?"

Most goldfish had a lifespan of about fifteen months, but for some unfathomable reason—thriving on the love in their house, maybe—Harvey lived on.

"Of course he misses you, honey." Gently, he removed her thumb from her mouth, and contemplated the feeling swelling inside his heart.

"Me, too?" Carly asked.

Carly, not so much, as she had been caught on several occasions on a chair beside the aquarium, face plastered against the glass, arm dangling in water, trying catch the poor fish.

"You, too, sweetheart," Daniel said, in what he had learned was one of those necessary lies of parenting.

Carly sighed her satisfaction, and burrowed deeper between him and Trixie. Daniel contemplated the sensation in his heart and the truth he had stumbled upon at the same time he had been trying to run away from it.

This was his truth: love was an arrow. A man ran from it, thinking it would do what arrows did, that it would pierce the flesh and bring nothing but pain and misery.

And yet, the magnificent irony was that a man needed to turn and face that arrow in flight, rip open his shirt and bare his chest to it.

He had to be afraid, and he had to do it, anyway.

So that he could know, that when that particular arrow shot from that particular bow, pierced his heart, it didn't bring death. It brought life.

"Daddy?"

A single word. How could one word hold so much? So much angst and responsibility and doubt? So much laughter and sweetness and unexpected moments of sheer delight? Such a fierce need to protect and keep safe? Such a desire to make the world better for his children and his children's children?

How could one word hold so much love?

"Daddy?"

There was a stillness inside him as he recognized the most beautiful of truths. He was the luckiest of men. In a world where it was so easy to take detours, to get distracted, to take wrong roads and never come back, Daniel had discovered the road that led him to the most important thing of all.

Daniel Riverton had discovered what he was born to do.

"Can you tell us a story?"

"Yes," he whispered over the lump in his throat, "Yes, I can."

* * * * *

#4415 THE RETURNING HERO
by Soraya Lane

When soldier Brett Palmer, Jamie's late husband's best friend, turns up on her doorstep, she *knows* it's fate. Could this be the second chance they've both been looking for?

#4416 ROAD TRIP WITH THE ELIGIBLE BACHELOR
by Michelle Douglas

When an airline strike interferes with their plans, Quinn Laverty reluctantly embarks on a road trip with (gorgeous!) politician Aidan. But will this be the most unexpected and life-changing journey of their lives?

#4417 SAFE IN THE TYCOON'S ARMS
by Jennifer Faye

Kate Whitley has asked for billionaire Lucas's help, and he can't refuse this beautiful stranger. Will this be the woman to see behind the headlines...and into his heart?

#4418 AWAKENED BY HIS TOUCH
by Nikki Logan

Corporate realizer Elliot may be on Laney's doorstep strictly for business, but as he begins to see life through her eyes, the chemistry between them becomes impossible to ignore....

LARGER-PRINT BOOKS!

GET 2 FREE LARGER-PRINT NOVELS PLUS
2 FREE GIFTS!

✦ HARLEQUIN®

Romance

From the Heart, For the Heart

YES! Please send me 2 FREE LARGER-PRINT Harlequin® Romance novels and my 2 FREE gifts (gifts are worth about $10). After receiving them, if I don't wish to receive any more books, I can return the shipping statement marked "cancel." If I don't cancel, I will receive 4 brand-new novels every month and be billed just $4.84 per book in the U.S. or $5.24 per book in Canada. That's a savings of at least 19% off the cover price! It's quite a bargain! Shipping and handling is just 50¢ per book in the U.S. and 75¢ per book in Canada.* I understand that accepting the 2 free books and gifts places me under no obligation to buy anything. I can always return a shipment and cancel at any time. Even if I never buy another book, the two free books and gifts are mine to keep forever.

119/319 HDN F43Y

Name	(PLEASE PRINT)

Address		Apt. #

City	State/Prov.	Zip/Postal Code

Signature (if under 18, a parent or guardian must sign)

Mail to the **Harlequin® Reader Service:**
IN U.S.A.: P.O. Box 1867, Buffalo, NY 14240-1867
IN CANADA: P.O. Box 609, Fort Erie, Ontario L2A 5X3
Want to try two free books from another line?
Call 1-800-873-8635 or visit www.ReaderService.com.

* Terms and prices subject to change without notice. Prices do not include applicable taxes. Sales tax applicable in N.Y. Canadian residents will be charged applicable taxes. Offer not valid in Quebec. This offer is limited to one order per household. Not valid for current subscribers to Harlequin Romance Larger-Print books. All orders subject to credit approval. Credit or debit balances in a customer's account(s) may be offset by any other outstanding balance owed by or to the customer. Please allow 4 to 6 weeks for delivery. Offer available while quantities last.

Your Privacy—The Harlequin® Reader Service is committed to protecting your privacy. Our Privacy Policy is available online at www.ReaderService.com or upon request from the Harlequin Reader Service.

We make a portion of our mailing list available to reputable third parties that offer products we believe may interest you. If you prefer that we not exchange your name with third parties, or if you wish to clarify or modify your communication preferences, please visit us at www.ReaderService.com/consumerchoice or write to us at Harlequin Reader Service Preference Service, P.O. Box 9062, Buffalo, NY 14269. Include your complete name and address.

HRLP13R

Enjoy this sneak preview of
THE RETURNING HERO,
the first in Soraya Lane's
THE SOLDIERS' HOMECOMING *duet!*

"LET ME STAY for a few days, let you catch up on some sleep while I'm here."

His voice was lower than usual, an octave deeper. She shook her head. "You don't have to do that. I'll be fine."

She might have been telling him no, but inside she was screaming out for him to stay. Having Brett here would make her feel safe, let her relax and just sleep solidly for a few nights at least, but she didn't expect him to do that.

And her intentions weren't pure, either. Because ever since she'd starting thinking about Brett in a certain way last night, remembering how soft his lips had been, how sensual it had been pressed against his body, she'd thought of nothing other than having him here. Keeping him close. Wondering if something could happen between them, and whether he wanted it as much as she did, even if she did know it was wrong.

"If I'm honest, Brett, having you here for a few days sounds idyllic." She wanted to stay strong, but she also wanted a man in her house again. Wanted the company of someone she could actually talk to, who wasn't afraid of the truth. Of what had happened to her husband. Because she had no one else to talk to, and no one else to turn to. She'd lost her dad and then her husband to war, and she was tired of being alone. "But only if you're sure."

She listened to Brett's big intake of breath, watched the way his body stiffened, then softened back to normal again.

"Then I'll stay. As long as you need me here, I'll stay."

She dropped her head to his shoulder. "He would have liked you being here. You know that, right?"

Brett shrugged, but she could tell he was finding this as awkward as she was. "You know, he made me promise to look out for you if anything ever happened to him. I just never figured that we'd actually be in that position."

Jamie smiled. "I'll never forget what you've done for me, Brett."

Brett was her friend. Nothing more. She just had to keep reminding herself of that, because falling in love with her husband's best buddy? Not something that could happen. Not now, not ever.

Brett could have been the man of her dreams—*once*. But now wasn't the time to look back. Now was about the future. The one she had to build without her husband by her side. No matter how much she was thinking about *that* kiss.

Don't miss THE RETURNING HERO by Soraya Lane, available March 2014. And look out for the second in this heartwarming duet, HER SOLDIER PROTECTOR, available April 2014.